Operation

Dokkaebi

Leon Michaels

Also by Leon Michaels

The Path Home

From the Mists of Darkness

Task Force Nemesis

"The Crane Equation Trilogy"

The Crane Equation: The Early Years

The Crane Equation: Rebuilding a Nation

The Crane Equation: The Crane Legacy

"The Black Ops Series"

Operation Damocles

Operation Dokkeabi

Operation Yofune-Nushi

Operation Kartikeya

The Black Orchid

To my wife of 45 years who reads my gibberish with questions

like:

"Why the dickens did you write this sentence this way?"

Dokkaebi: From Korean folklore, a type of demon or orge.

These creatures love mischief and playing mean tricks on bad

people.

ACT I

A Walk in the Woods

Moving through the leaves and debris of a forest floor without making noise is a trait few ever master. Dry leaves rustle and small twigs crack as the person places one foot in front of the other as they move from one point to another. If you wish to call it a trick, the trick is to move your feet in such a way as not to disturb the leaves or snap the twigs. It is almost like a ballet dancer moving across a stage, flowing with the music.

Tonight, in the woods of Fort Leonard Wood Missouri, a test was being ran by a single individual, code named Blue, to see if they could move undetected to a dummy supply cache and simulate blowing it up. Blue had parachuted into the Army Base just before daylight from a Blackhawk helicopter from one thousand feet to a landing zone marked by a single, infrared marker. For Blue, this was the tenth jump for record utilizing a para-wing and night vision goggles to guide them into the LZ.

From the LZ, Blue had to move thirty kilometers to the cache site, destroy it, then evade to the pickup point where one of the instructors would pick Blue up and finish the test. If Blue could not be picked up, then Blue had to move to a second location, ten kilometers from the cache to find safety and finish the test. The second location was considered a 'safe house'.

The intelligence package for this test was incomplete in that what was not given was that two Missouri National Guard Infantry Battalions were doing their Annual Training camps at that time and were positioned in the field doing a field training exercise between the cache site and the pick-up point. The National Guard units had been warned that it was possible that Special Forces troops could be working in the area as Opposing Forces, aka The Enemy, and try to infiltrate the National Guard positions as part of their own training exercises. Except that Blue was not part of the Special Forces or even a member of the U.S. Army.

The cache was being guarded by trainees from the U.S. Army's Military Police School located on Fort Leonard Wood as part of their normal training. Every night a duty roster was exercised with those on the roster being awakened, taken to a location and stand guard for two hours, and then returned to their bunks to get what remained of their sleep before beginning a new day of training to become Military Police. These trainees were not aware of the Special Forces training exercises in the area. They ignored the Guard exercises and the Guard had this location marked as Off Limits on their training maps.

Blue had been moving on the target since landing at the LZ at 0500 hours. Thirty kilometers in a straight-line distance did not apply since Blue had to make detours at every turn to keep out of sight of the normal, daily happenings in the training areas. Exhaustion was closing in on Blue's body, but the end was almost in sight. Blue took another compass bearing and estimated it was only three hundred meters to the target. If the school had kept their schedule, a new sentry had been posted just minutes earlier, fresh from a warm bed and probably a bit groggy. Thirty to forty-five minutes to close the distance, then recon the target before moving in and setting a dummy charge on the cache then moving on to the pickup point.

As Blue closed on the target, the sentry made things easier for them by tapping on the empty wood crates stacked at the cache. Sitting on the crates was the sentry playing a poor version of Queen's We Will Rock You with drum sticks made of dead limbs found around the area. The only light at the cache was a battery powered lantern. Blue smiled and decided to take advantage of the situation. Blue reset the timer on the dummy bomb and moved around the cache, coming in behind the stack of crates and placing the bomb between two of the crates. Slowly Blue moved back from the stack of crates and placed another bomb where it would not do any real damage when it blew. The first device would make a loud whistling then generate a large smoke cloud without setting anything on fire while the second device would create an explosion equal to approximately one quarter pound of TNT. This second device was a modified artillery simulator used by the military in training. Both devices would go off at 0200 when a changing of the guard should catch the oncoming sentry along with the off going sentry.

Movement to the pickup point was not without hazard when Blue nearly stumbled into a three-man National Guard listening post. Using the night vision goggles, Blue was able to skirt the LP, then move through the lines of dug in Infantry, avoiding the training warning devices rigged in front of their positions. It was slow going but no alarm was sounded, and Blue reached the pickup point along the trail to the cache in time to see the pickup truck taking the new sentry out to the cache.

Blue pulled the protective covered from their watch and smiled when exactly at 0200 hours the sound of the explosive device was heard echoing through the woods from the bottom up to the ridge the trail was on. Almost immediately the National Guard Companies became alert and in a few minutes Blue could hear the sounds of patrols moving about, searching for intruders. Blue carefully moved across the trail a minute before the pickup moved back to the main base. Blue had turned on the tactical radio utilizing an earbud to keep the noise down and heard nothing but static. No call from the individual that was to pick them up.

Blue pulled the Garmin GPS from their vest, took a reading then hung it from a tree limb. The Garmin had a locator in it which would give its position away the moment it was turned on which was why Blue had used a compass during the test. Blue had set a bearing into the Garmin leading in a different direction from the safe house and moved out into the darkness. The going was slow and twice Blue had to evade patrols as the distance to the safe house closed as daylight approached. It was important to reach the safe house in the darkness otherwise Blue would have to vanish back into the woods during the day until night fall. Being alone meant sleep would be a high-risk situation, even well back into the woods.

The end was in visual sight with barely thirty minutes of darkness left but there was also nearly one hundred meters of open ground between the woods and safety. Blue pulled everything tight to the body, slung their silenced MP-5 behind the back and began a long slow crawl to safety. At the edge of the street separating danger from safety Blue stopped beside a pickup truck and waited for a second before springing up and sprinting to the door, opening it and stepping in, slamming the door closed. Inside were four people and they just stared at the person who had just abruptly entered the room? Three were instructors and one, a black gentleman, was a person Blue did not know.

"Damn!" Spoke one of the instructors as he took his wallet from his trousers, removed what appeared to be a one-hundred dollar bill and handed it to another instructor who took it and removed a money clip from their pocket, peeled off several bills, placing them on the coffee mess before putting the larger bill into the clip and back into their pocket.

"Congratulations Megan. That is your share of the bet."

Megan Ann Wagner looked at the money but focused on the coffee pot as she walked to it, poured herself a cup and just scooped up the money and crammed it into the pocket of her lizard stripped field uniform. She walked over to a table, placed the cup of coffee on it as she began to pull her gear off her exhausted body. When she pulled her goggles from her bandana covered head, leafy twigs fell to the floor that had been wedged in the headband to break up the outline of her head. She sat down and sipped on the hot coffee knowing her debrief would take place before she could get cleaned up and get some sleep.

The black gentleman only announced himself as the Chief Evaluator of this test as he opened the file on Megan Wagner and looked at the photo inside. She looked like a woman who should be walking the runway modeling Victoria's Secret instead of sitting before him in filthy camouflage clothing and a face smudged from matching makeup to hide her features. Her hair was nearly pitch black showing her Sioux and Okinawan heritage and it was cut in a pixie cut so as not to be a problem for training. She stood five foot seven inches and her last weight-in showed her to weight one hundred and twenty-eight pounds. Megan reminded him of another female operator he had worked with a few years earlier and knew looks could be deceiving.

During her debrief, she never mentioned the actions of the sentry figuring the shock of the devices going off would teach him to be more alert in their sentry duties than having a Drill Sergeant chewing on his butt for an hour or two. The Evaluator never gave his name during the debrief, and once completed, she was taken to the Post's Bachelor Officer's Quarters where she showered and finally relaxed, falling asleep with her hair still wet. She had eaten hot rations brought in from a mess hall while being debriefed, slept through lunch and ate dinner at the Officer's Club before boarding an airplane back to Virginia and the CIA's Training Facility commonly known as The Farm.

What she was never told was that she was the only individual to complete their mission without getting detected or caught. Five others were tested during that same time frame at various military posts across the country. Some were detected before they reached their objective and others were captured after setting their charges.

A week after the test, Megan returned to her room after morning physical training to find an envelope taped to her room door. In it were her car keys which she had surrendered at the start of the course and her travel instructions along with orders for her next assignment. This was her graduation. After she had her car packed, she turned in her room key and was given another envelope. This one contained her CIA credentials and a map guiding her to a furnished apartment already allocated for her use along with the keys to the apartment. She was told further instructions would be found within the apartment concerning her next assignment.

Megan Ann Wagner was twenty-three years of age and looked more Asian than Native American. Her father met her mother while stationed on Okinawa at Island Headquarters with the U.S. Army. Horace G. Wagner was a Special Forces Staff

Sergeant who had been wounded during Operation Desert Storm and this overseas tour was as much a recuperation tour of duty as he was getting back in shape to return to Special Forces. Megan's mother, Aimeko, was the brother of an instructor at a Karate Dojo which Horace was attending to further his knowledge and help rebuild his battered body. After months of courting Aimeko, following native tradition, they were first married in a traditional Okinawan ceremony then that after noon in a Christian ceremony at the base chapel.

Aimeko became pregnant with Megan on their wedding night and Horace requested an extension of tour on Okinawa so the infant would be born on the island with Aimeko's parents attending. Megan was born in the U.S. Army Hospital at Camp Kuwee. Megan was raised speaking three languages, English, Sioux of her father's people and the Okinawan version of Japanese. Every time Horace was deployed overseas for a long tour of duty, Aimeko took Megan back to Okinawa to be with her grandparents and relatives. Her Uncle began at an early age teaching her GoJuRu, the Okinawan version of Karate and when home, Horace continued her education in the form as he had attained a Second Degree Black belt.

Megan was early in her sophomore year at the University of North Carolina when she was recruited by the CIA and transferred to Georgetown University for her junior year to earn a degree in International Studies paid for by the CIA. She soon discovered that she disagreed with nearly all of the liberal teachings at Georgetown and her research for papers reinforced her disagreement. Her father told her to go with the 'School solution' and keep her disgust and disagreement inside as she moves through her education, but to remember and hold her own beliefs high in her dealings with other people.

With her looks Megan had suitors at her heels since she blossomed out at age thirteen and had her pick of lovers during college. Megan enjoyed sex but knew that it was only a relief from the stress of college and tried not to allow it to distract her from her education. At Georgetown she almost became celibate because it seemed all the men who hit on her were full of their own worth with egos matching the expensive cars they drove. Megan was never interested in other females and she noticed the only real difference between the two sexes at Georgetown was their sexual plumbing. Even the boys she had enjoyed in High School had moved on, most married so when she entered her new apartment, she had been celibate for nearly two years.

Megan learned once in her apartment that she was to report to the State Department for training as a files clerk as part of her CIA cover once assigned overseas. In the instructions she found in an envelope at the apartment was dress code guidance and Megan spent the next day shopping for the proper clothing as required for the course. When she checked into the course location, she turned in her clothing receipts for reimbursement as per a clothing allowance.

The course was simple in concept as it was designed for personal with less than a full college education. Megan moved through the course without difficulty other than being hit on at least once a week. She knew how she looked to others but her parents had kept her grounded in the reality that what truly made a person beautiful came from the inside, not from the exterior body. This affected her in several ways as she picked friends and lovers. Her standards were high, and she lived up to those standards as her friends would always discover. Megan did date several men during the course but none of them found their way into her bed.

Once the clerical course was completed, Megan was tested on her language skills. She had taken Farsi in college as part of her International Studies and was tested on it along with her Japanese. Her knowledge of her Sioux was never noted in her files and she never gave that information away to her interviewers. Once her testing was complete, Megan was informed she was heading to the U.S. Army's Language School in California to study Korean for her first field assignment.

Megan was tested once again at the language school and was passed on her Japanese. She was given an updated course in

Farsi then on to the Korean language. One day in the cafeteria, she spurned the advances of another student who decided to curse her in Swahili. She rose from her chair and backed the man half way across the room as she was speaking in Lakota. Several instructors took notice of this unknown language at the school and she was later interviewed by the school commandant concerning the incident and the language she used. Megan advised the commandant of what she was speaking, and they interview ended a notation in her school records of an additional language.

When not studying, Megan was either running or working out in the school's exercise facility. She had run cross-country in high school and had maintained her exercise routine whenever ever possible. Megan loved to swim and learned years before as much as she preferred a two-piece bathing suit, a one piece caused her less trouble with the opposite sex. She also kept her karate exercises up, maintaining her skills on the punching bags.

Megan was not able to get any range time in since she had not been allowed to bring her issued Sig P250 with her to the language school. She would smile to herself every time she thought about her first time on the pistol range at the Farm; the instructor picked her out because of her looks thinking she was the weak one in the group. He went through a precise set of instructions even a five-year old could understand about what he wanted her to do as they were starting with a man size silhouette at ten meters. Megan's Sig was in a hip holster, unloaded as per instructions. He told her to draw her weapon, loaded it and shoot at target number five. When he told her to go, she was removing a magazine from the pouch on her left hip as the Sig was being drawn from her right. Megan inserted the magazine and worked the slide on the pistol as she was moving into a modified Weaver shooting position. She placed three rounds into the head of the target with all three bullet holes touching.

She holstered the pistol and asked the instructor if that was what he had in mind. The instructor was upset and told her to do it again. Megan was drawing the Sig as she turned on the target and emptied the other ten rounds she had in the magazine in the same tight group. Her class laughed as they saw the hole in the target slightly enlarge as she dropped the magazine, catching in in mid-air and putting it back in her magazine pouch.

Megan's father had taught her to shoot as soon as she was old enough to hold a pistol and small rifle starting with .22 caliber finally graduating to 44 Magnums by the time she was fifteen. He taught her every trick a sniper should know by the time she finished high school and she had even shot on the Army's ranges with members of her father's Special Forces team at ranges out to one thousand meters.

Her abilities to move in the field came from hours moving in the woods with her father hunting or bird watching. She learned to survive in every environment as he took her camping every weekend he had free and later she was joined by a younger brother as he learned to enjoy the outdoors. Megan had learned mountaineering in the same Georgia Mountains that the Army Rangers trained in and the swamps of Southern Georgia and Florida taught her how to stay alive in places only desperate men went.

Megan's karate skills also surprised the instructors since she had left that information off her biography she had to fill in when she was approached by the CIA. Once Megan was in school, she no longer went back to Okinawa when her father was deployed but during the summer she was sent when her mother could not travel due to being pregnant with one of her two younger brothers. Her uncle had his own karate school by this time and she spent hours in his Dojo watching and learning. He never allowed her to be part of a class but taught her in private before or after the school was open. Her father carried her training on when he was home as he now had a Second Degree Black Belt.

During the first two hand to hand combat classes she watched the instructor take advantage of his position and grope a couple of the other female students while making hands on corrections or giving personal instruction. On the third day she volunteered to be the student dummy and she was told to execute a specific punch at him and he was going to show the class how to block it. Megan knew several ways to block the punch but felt he was going to do a take-down which would give him plenty of her body to grope as he grappled with her. She threw the punch and he reacted as she figured he would, but before he could get control of her, she had him on the ground with her in command and had dislocated his shoulder in doing so as she stood above him smiling.

The Director of Instruction had her standing before his desk demanding an explanation. She just told him what she had observed and was not about to allow him to lay hands on her. When she was asked what her rating was in karate, she told them she had never been tested or rated. Her complete records to include the investigation of her mother's family was examined along with her father's service records before they came to realize she was probably a First Degree Black Belt or even higher. It was during this examination of records that they found out her father's last assignment. He was a member of Delta Force for the last eight years of his Army career.

Megan finished the language school without any personal involvement with staff or other students even thought she had gone out once with an Army Sergeant who was there learning German and if he had asked her out another time or two, she might have shared a bed with him. She returned to her apartment and was given her first assignment. Megan was headed to Seoul Korea under the credentials of a State Department employee. She packed up her apartment separating the things that would be shipped to Korea and took two weeks with her parents at their small farm outside Spring Lake, North Carolina just four miles from the North-East edge of Fort Bragg.

Stilettos are not just Heels

Because of her Asian looks and her language abilities, Megan spent a lot of time moving around Korea in her cover of Assistant to the Attaché for Agriculture and Horticulture. She studied both subjects in order to be literate in the subjects as she collected information from local agents. The rules prohibited her from being armed but Megan wore long sleeved dresses or blouses with sleeves open enough no one ever caught on to the fact she wore a ceramic stiletto in a nylon sheath on her left forearm and often an additional one on her right calf if wearing slacks.

Megan even wore these knives when traveling to Japan as a courier and because of their composition; they were never discovered by metal detectors. One of her duties in Japan was to inspect agriculture cargo in Japan before it was shipped to Korea to insure the United States was getting their monies worth. She was always escorted by one of the embassy's Marine Security Detachment in civilian clothes and also like her, they were not allowed to carry a firearm during those trips to the Tokyo docks warehouses. The Marines who escorted her liked her because unlike many of the State Department personal they had to deal with, she treated them with respect and often bought them lunch at one of the seafood restaurants near the docks.

She was sixteen months into a three-year assignment when things began a disturbing trend. Twice she had gone out on her monthly tours around Korea and each time an agent failed to make their meet. Two Korean agents had gone missing without any indication of foul play. They just seemed to fall off the face of the earth. Her CIA supervisor was an experienced field officer and he told her to be careful the next time she went out.

A week after her last tour, Megan was sent to Japan to assist in processing a cargo of rice seed of a new breed of rice which was disease resistant to a fungus slowly moving across Korea, destroying hectares of rice. After a thorough review of the shipping documents, she was escorted to the warehouse where the cargo of seed was being stored prior to shipment. Her escort was a

Marine Lance Corporal named Conley who stood close to six feet tall with a solid build and appeared to be older than the average Marine of his rank. Megan thought he looked out of place in a sport coat, and slacks with his high and tight Marine haircut. He seemed a bit nervous around her but as they talked during the ride to the warehouse in the back of the embassy car driven by a Japanese driver, she found he had only been in Japan for less than two months and on his first assignment out of the State Department School that Marines attend prior to being posted to an embassy.

The first thing Megan noticed as they entered the warehouse was the absence of warehouse workers. She checked her watch, did the math since it was still set for Seoul and saw it was not the normal break time for these workers. They found the three stacks of seed and began to inventory and check the tags on the bags to insure each bag was accounted for. The cargo had not yet been plastic wrapped for shipment which made it easier for this task. She was just starting to inventory the second stack when the hairs on the back of her neck told her something was really wrong here.

Megan closed her mind to block out any outside noise. This was a trick her father had taught her nearly a decade ago and she often practiced it as a way to clear her mind. Within seconds she heard a slight sound, a sound of feet moving across the concrete floor, barely scrapping the floor in a slow movement. She heard another she could not place but it was above them and near the third stack of seed. Megan took a quick look around as she carefully removed the stiletto from her arm and placed it under her clipboard, hiding it from prying eyes. She moved close to Conley and whispered in his ear.

"Heads up Marine, things are about to get nasty. Stay close and follow me."

Conley had a surprised look on his face as he followed Megan out to a center aisle where they had more room to maneuver if needed. As tempting as it was for him to enjoy the view of following Megan as the skirt of her dress swished back and forth, but his head was swiveling around to watch for some danger she must have detected. He was also wishing he had his M9 Beretta with him.

They had barely reached the center of the aisle when the first group of men came from around a stack of crates in front of them. There were three men and they were not dressed as warehouse workers. The second group came from the back side of the seed stacks and spread out. There were also three in this group.

"Miss Wagner, we have three men behind us."

"I know, you stay close and deal with them while I handle these men. Stay loose and let them come to you."

Conley reached into his pocket and found his cell phone. This phone was specially constructed with a pop-off rubber cap which covered a button that when pushed sent a signal back to the Security Detachment's Radio Room alerting them to the carrier of that phone to be in danger.

The first man to approach Megan had a sick grin on his face and as he closed the distance he pulled a long knife from inside his jacket. He told her he was going to cut her clothes off her then they were going to enjoy raping her before tossing her off the dock with her throat cut. Megan laughed as she dropped the clipboard. His eyes started to follow the clipboard to the floor before he realized she was closing in on him. He tried to slash at her with the knife, but she blocked his arm and stepped close enough to kiss him as she drove her stiletto up under his ribs, twisted the blade then moved it left to right ripping the bottom of his heart apart.

Megan pulled the knife out of his body and stepped aside to let him fall away from her to the floor. Conley heard the knife hit the floor and looked down to see it slide a bit past him. He bent over and scooped it up. As he was rising back up two of the men on his side attacked him with clubs. He drove the knife into the chest of the nearest man and barely dodged the swing of the other man's club as it glanced off his left shoulder. He turned into his

13

attacker and as the man was recovering to take another swing, Conley caught him with a punishing right cross, knocking him on his back and out of action. Conley picked up the dead man's club and stood waiting for the third man.

The other two men to Megan's front came at her with clubs. She had heard the commotion behind her but when she heard Conley let out a yell at whoever was left behind her; she knew he was still in the fight. She took the man to her left as she blocked his swing and drove her knife up into his throat as she was pushing him into the other man, blocking his ability to swing at her. As she turned on him, she could see Conley engaging his opponent but focused on her last man. Her knife was lodged in the man's throat and she went after the third man bare handed.

He took a downward swing at her which she blocked with both hands, kicked him in the groin, and then wrenched the club from his hands. In one motion she pivoted and caught him in the ear with the heel of her flat, then hit him again in the back of his head with the club as he was going down. Megan turned to see Conley choking his opponent with a club across the throat as blood was flowing down the side of his head. Conley had taken a hard hit but had stayed in the fight. Megan stepped around in front of Conley and looked at his opponent.

"At ease Marine, he's dead."

Conley looked up at Megan then back down at the man he had in his grasp before letting go of him. Conley just rocked back on his heels and sat down on the floor.

"Miss Wagner, what the hell just happened here?"

"What's your given name Marine?"

"James, Ma'am."

"Call me Megan. I'm not sure what happened but I think it is time to call for the cavalry."

Conley pulled the cell phone from his pocket and looked at the window. He showed it to Megan.

"I pushed the panic button Megan. It shows received which means the cavalry is on the way."

Megan squatted down and looked into his eyes.

"Stand up James and try to focus. This may not be over yet and if you allow yourself to go to sleep, you may not wake up."

Megan helped him up and with some effort, pulled the knife from the man's chest and handed it to him. She went to get hers from her opponent's throat and finally decided it was not coming out. She picked up a club and then went back to Conley, and basically held him up as sirens could be heard coming closer. Megan looked down at her dress and saw it was covered with blood as were her hands and arms. It was then she wondered where the embassy's driver was at. But they were far enough into the warehouse he might not have heard ruckus. She heard footsteps running towards them and shook Conley.

"Heads up James, we have company coming."

"I'm trying Megan, but damn my head hurts."

The first person Megan saw was wearing the uniform of a security guard as the sirens stopped. Moments later, police officers swarmed the warehouse. Megan dropped the club and had to remove the knife from James' hand. He was groggy but was trying to stay on his feet. He kept muttering he had to protect her.

Megan just held onto James as a Japanese Police Lieutenant came up to her and asked her what had happened. She explained her identification was in their embassy car which at that time she was told the driver was lying in the back seat with his throat cut. Megan estimated the man who came at her with the knife had killed the driver before they came after her and James. Paramedics arrived a few minutes later and took charge of James, relieving her of the responsibility. She told them how he received his injury but not how hard he had been hit.

As the Paramedics were taking Conley out on a gurney, a four-man Marine reaction team arrived accompanied by the Security Detachment's Commanding Officer. A few minutes behind him was the resident FBI agent for the embassy. Her purse was recovered from the car and she showed her State Department identification which gave her diplomatic immunity. The police Lieutenant surveyed the scene and determine because of the tattoos the men were wearing that the immunity was not necessary. Of the six men who had attacked them, five were dead and one was still unconscious from James' fist.

Megan gave the FBI agent a detailed breakdown of what had happened who then asked the Japanese Police to taken plenty of photos of the crime scene including Megan covered in blood. Megan was then placed in the care of the reaction team and escorted back to the embassy where she took a long, hot shower to remove all the blood from her body. Her clothes were placed in a plastic bag she had been given and they would in turn be given to the Japanese police. She cleaned her arm sheath and replaced the lost blade with a spare she carried in her luggage.

Once cleaned up, Megan was escorted to one of the small meeting rooms where she was interviewed concerning the incident. The resident FBI agent handled the interview with the resident CIA officer and the Marine Security Detachment Commander present to witness the interview. The interview was both videoed and a stenographer took a written account of the interview. It was not until the interview was over that anyone other than the FBI agent asked questions. Megan had been read her rights prior to the first question and answered each question as accurate as possible.

Megan did ask about the condition of Conley once the interview was over and insured that within her statements, she gave credit to Conley for dealing with the men he faced. Once the interview was over, she asked the Marine officer if it would be improper to write a letter of commendation to be entered into

Conley's service records. She was told if she wrote one, he would insure it was entered into his records. Megan spent nearly an hour forming and writing the letter, signing it under her State Department identification.

The Ambassador to Japan called her into his office after reviewing her written account of the interview and informed her that the Japanese Police had been in contact with the embassy and no charges would be pressed against her. Both actions by her and Lance Corporal Conley were considered self-defense. She was to pack her bags and would be taken to the airport and placed on a plane back to Korea within the hour. Megan had already packed knowing they would want her out of the country as soon as possible. Within the hour, Megan was on an Air Force diplomatic aircraft enroute to Kimpo Airfield.

James Conley had suffered a concussion from the blow to the side of his head along with the need for eight stitches to close the wound from the blow. The Japanese police had an officer standing outside his room for the first three days he was in the hospital then had the officer replaced by a hospital security officer. It was late in the evening on his fourth day in the hospital when a fight occurred in the hall outside his room. The security officer noticed the doctor attempting to enter his room was wearing shoes that were scuffed and dirty and asked for his identification. The fake doctor attempted to run but the security officer, having retired from the police, was able to subdue him and it was found he was carrying a syringe filled with an exotic poison. He also had the tattoos of the gang that had attacked Megan and Conley. James had had several Marine visitors during his stay and one had managed to sneak a switchblade to him, which James had in his hand as he listened to the fight in the hallway. Two hours later, Conley was transferred to the embassy to finish his recovery under the care of the embassy doctor then a week later, flown to Hawaii for another week before being placed on medical leave before being reassigned to a new duty assignment.

Megan was never officially admonished for carrying the stiletto, but her CIA supervisor did remind her she was not to be armed during the performance of her duties unless it was proscribed due to the nature of the duties. He never told her she could not carry her stiletto, but her duties were reduced until Langley determined her status based on the reports being filed.

Word had reached the Seoul Marine Detachment from Tokyo about the incident and her actions during it and they held a small ceremony issuing a certificate to Megan making her an Honorary Devil Dog. Megan just went with the normal routine of office work as she waited for determination of her operational status. About the only interesting thing Megan could discover during her wait was that she seemed to have attracted the attention of the Marine Security Detachments Executive Officer. Megan found him interesting but not enough to become romantically involved with him.

Megan was invited to the Detachment's Marine Corps Birthday Ball at the end of the week and as she was walking to her shared apartment with her roommate, Linda, who worked as a Visa Clerk, trouble once again, reared its head. They were talking about what to wear since Linda was dating one of the Marine Sergeants when Megan almost missed the gunman.

The gunman was in the back seat of a cab coming up the street as they walked on the sidewalk. Linda was nearest the street but was not looking at the street in front of them. Megan saw the gunman's AK-47 as he leaned out the car window to fire upon them. Megan pulled Linda down with her as she dropped to the sidewalk just as the gunman started shooting. When the shooting started, the driver saw the two women going down and thought the deed was done and accelerated the car causing the gunman to fire wildly.

Megan heard Linda cry out as bullets impacted all around them as the cab passed them heading away from them. As the car sped away it was heading to the embassy's employee port of entry guarded by two armed Marines. They reacted to the shooting by stepping out to the edge of the street with their M9 Beretta's drawn. The gunman was still trying to fire on the women lying on the sidewalk as the two Marines opened fire on the driver and gunman moving towards them. Megan felt something sting her right thigh as the last burst of fire was directed at her and Linda. She could hear the sound of the Marines 9mm Beretta's firing mixed with the sound of the AK-47.

The driver was hit four times and crashed the cab across the street from the Marines who continued to fire upon the assailants. The gunman tried to turn on the Marines with his weapon but was hit a total of nine times before the Marines ceased fire. They closed on the car as other Marines poured out of the employee entrance heavily armed for combat.

Megan reached over Linda to roll her over and felt moisture at her side. She removed her hand and looked at it covered in blood. She then rose up and looked back up the street to the entrance and saw three Marines running in her direction. Megan raised her bloody hand in the air for the Marines to see and one stopped, turned back to the entranced and called for a Corpsman. She started to get up and then felt a sharp pain in her leg where she had moments before felt the sting. Megan looked down at her leg and saw blood soaking the light blue skirt she was wearing. She just lay back down and waited.

The Corpsman arrived moments later as the Marines stood guard over the women. Megan told the Corpsman to deal with Linda first as she just waited her turn. One of the Marines, a Corporal dropped to his knees besides Megan, raised her skirt to see how bad her injury was to her leg. He quickly removed his tie and used it as a tourniquet to slow the flow of blood from her leg. The Corpsman was working hard as he was bandaging Linda's wound when he noticed what the Corporal was doing with Megan. He quickly reached into his aid bag and tossed a wound dressing to the Corporal who went back to work, sealing her wound and protecting it.

The street became crowded as armed Marines filled it along with Korean police responding to the shooting. Marines had pulled the bodies of the cab driver and shooter from the cab and they were lying, stretched out on the ground beside the car. The embassy's doctor came to the women and got the report from the Corpsman on their condition. He ordered Megan taken into the embassy's dispensary, but Linda transported to the Air Force Hospital at Kimpo Airfield. A second Corpsman arrived carrying a major trauma bag and IV's were started in Linda.

One of the Marines guarding the women scooped Megan up in his arms and headed back to the embassy with her with the doctor leading the way. She was taken to a small surgery suite and placed on the table and her dress cut away from her as an IV was started. A portable x-ray machine was moved to take a picture of what was in the leg and soon the doctor came to her with the film in hand.

"Miss Wagner, it seems that you have a piece of the copper jacket from a bullet in your thigh. I'm going to give you a local at the wound site and see if I can get it out without doing more damage to the exterior of your leg."

"Alright doctor, do what you have to do."

Fifteen minutes later the doctor was sewing up her wound after removing a jagged piece of the copper jacket from her thigh. Megan asked if she could keep the piece of metal and the doctor placed it into a small medicine bottle for her. She was moved to one of the four beds in the infirmary, given a shot to make her go to sleep and a Marine posted outside the door of the clinic.

Megan awoke to a need to void her bladder. Her IV was gone and she was now wearing a hospital gown that she had no memory of having been put into. There was a small bathroom in her room and she hobbled into it and used the facilities then back into bed. Her personal things were on the table next to her bed and she picked up her watch to see it was eight thirty-seven, but the watch did not have a date indicator, so she did not know if it was morning or evening. She just sat on the bed waiting, feeling the ache of the wound to her leg trying to figure out not only what had actually happened but why it happened. She finally decided to find out what was happening out in the world and opened the door to her room to find herself looking at the back of a Marine. The Marine turned to look at her.

"Miss Wagner, shouldn't you be in bed ma'am?"

"Probably Marine, but I'm hungry and would like to know how Miss Webster is doing."

"Please return to bed ma'am. I'll pass the word that you are up and see about getting you some chow."

Megan returned to bed and waited. It wasn't long before the doctor knocked on the door then entered followed by a nurse carrying a tray with bandage materials. He removed the wrap from her leg and looked at the wound before applying Betadine around the injury then rewrapping it. As he was finishing up, a Marine entered with another tray and she could see it had covered dishes on it along with on small box of fruit juice. He sat in on the moveable hospital table and moved it to where she could get to it. He never spoke to her, but she did thank him for bringing the tray to her.

Word came down that Linda had survived her wound and would be transported back to the states within the week. Megan was heavily escorted to her apartment on the third day after the shooting to supervise packing of her property for shipment back to the states. She was returning home as soon as transportation could be arranged. Megan spent a week in the small clinic room before she was taken to Kimpo and placed on a C-17 transport aircraft and returned to the states dressed as a Marine in a set of digitals.

Other than moving about the aircraft during flight, Megan was not allowed to leave the aircraft the two times it landed dropping off cargo or picking additional cargo up for further transport. Her leg was stiff, and she was told not to attempt exercise for another week to allow her wound to heal without ripping the stitches out. She deplaned at Pope Air Force base and was examined by an Air Force doctor and changed into civilian clothes. Her parents had been notified of her return and were able to visit with her for an hour before she was loaded up in a government Denali and headed for the Farm. Megan had been instructed to tell anyone outside the CIA that she had been injured in an automobile accident. Her father just grinned that knowing grin he had when he knew the line he was being fed was pure bullshit.

Megan was approaching her twenty-sixth birthday as she returned to where it all started for her, The Farm. No romantic interest in her life and she had been celibate since she had transferred to Georgetown. But she had questions concerning both the warehouse incident and the drive-by shooting that were not being satisfied by the official statements on both incidents.

Clowns with Machineguns!!

Megan had nothing to do at the Farm except think. After a week she began to formulate a theory concerning both incidents based on what little knowledge she had and finally constructed a letter to the Director of Operations concerning her theory. She did get a note back saying he had received the letter and had taken it under consideration. By this time, Megan was doing light exercises to get the stiffness out of her leg and was jogging to rebuild the damaged muscle in it.

With the time on her hands to expend, she was able to check out a Sig P250 from the Farm's armory and spent hours on the pistol range burning up as much ammunition as they would allow keeping her ability to shoot up to her father's standards. There was another group of students at the Farm and she avoided them as much as possible. Megan was restricted to the Farm even though her car had been brought down from her parent's place where it was being stored while in Korea.

Megan returned from her morning run and found a note on her door. It only said to be ready for the range and she would be picked up at 0900. Megan showered, changed and went to eat then returned to her room and waited. She was reading the newest Clive Cussler novel when there was a sharp rap on her door. Looking at the clock on her nightstand she saw it was nine o'clock. Megan put the book down and went to open the door. Opening it she was greeted with the view of a woman she estimated to be in her mid to late thirties, black hair, dark eyes and roughly the same height she was. Her facial features appeared Middle East.

"Megan Wagner I presume?" She spoke in flawless Farsi without an accent.

"Yes. You are correct. And you are?"

"Just call me Janice. Do you have your range bag packed?"

"Yes, I am ready to go."

"Holsters in the bag?"

"Yes, both belt and drop leg."

"Good, grab your jacket and bag and let's go. The clock is running."

Janice just stood looking at her until Megan went for her range bag and jacket lying on her bed. Megan realized the entire conversation had been in Farsi. If Megan had not seen the CIA identification card hanging from a strap around Janice's neck she might have been concerned about leaving with her. Megan locked her room and followed Janice out to the parking lot. When Janice walked to a white Range Rover, Megan noticed it had a Marine Officers Decal on the front bumper allowing it to enter Marine bases and it had no state vehicle license plate on the front, instead it had a scarlet plate with a gold Marine Corps emblem embossed on it. Janice told her to put her bag in the back seat and when Megan opened the rear passenger door the sight of a child's car seat took her by surprise. Megan got into the front seat, buckled up and waited for the next surprise.

The surprise came when Janice turned towards the main gate of the Farm instead of to the ranges. The gate guard just opened the gate as they drove up to it without checking the vehicle or passengers as per procedure. Janice acted as if this was normal procedure and just focused on her driving as they entered the highway system.

"May I ask where we are going?" Megan asked in English.

"We are going to have some fun." Janice replied in English. Megan noticed a slight Mid-Western accent in her English.

Megan finally got a good look at Janice's left hand and noticed her ring finger was devoid of rings, but there was the indentation and lightness of skin color where wedding rings would be worn. Megan deduced that Janice had removed recently her rings and spent a lot of time in the sun due to the differences in skin tone. Megan just sat back and relaxed figuring she would be told more at the proper time.

It caught Megan off guard when they turned into one of the secondary gates to the Quantico Marine Corps Base. Janice drove through the base finally pulling in front of a large metal building with a sign next to the door announcing this to be the Tactical Indoor Shooting Facility. Janice looked at Megan and smiled.

"This is also called The Funhouse. Grab your gear and let's go have some fun."

Megan retrieved her bag from the back seat as Janice went to the rear of the rover and opened it up. With her bag in hand, Megan walked to the back of the Rover as Janice closed the back and Megan got a look at the license plate on the vehicle. Seeing the plate, she learned that Oklahoma only required a single license plate unlike a majority of states. She followed Janice into the building and down a hall to a small room where another woman was waiting. The woman greeted Janice with a hug and a kiss to the cheek.

"Janice, thank you for coming. I hope the men can do without you for a couple days."

"Dotty, Jonathan told his father he wanted to go fishing so Jake packed the truck and off they went."

Dotty laughed.

"I can just see the Gunner with his heels locked taking orders from a five-year old!"

Dotty turned to look at Megan and stepped to her with an offered hand.

"Miss Wagner, my name is Dorothy, but my friends call me Dotty. Gear up, we have this place for only two hours and we have a lot of work to do."

Megan noticed Dotty was wearing a pistol on her right hip, so she began to gear up accordingly.

"How many magazines Dotty?"

"One locked and four in reserve. If you have them, stick a couple in your back pocket just in case Master Sergeant Peters has rigged the game."

"Who is Master Sergeant Peters?"

Janice and Dotty laughed.

"He's a retired Marine who taught Dotty how to shoot." Answered Janice.

"And he has an evil sense of humor when he's sober." Added Dotty.

Janice had taken her jacket off and adjusted her pull-over sweater to provide clearance to her holster and ammunition pouches. Megan laid her gear out on a table in the corner of the room and quickly assembled herself before walking over to the main table and loading her magazines from the open ammo can on it. Soon she was ready to go.

"Dotty, are you sure you should be doing this?"

"Janice, I'm only three months along and I have a vest on under my sweater just to keep Dave happy. Besides, I've seen you shoot and according to Jackson, Megan here is even better than you ever were. So, let's get this done."

Dotty led them down a different hall until they reached a closed door. She paused and looked a Megan.

"Miss Wagner, I hope you do not mind me calling you Megan because from this point on, Miss Wagner takes too much time and time is very important on the other side of this door. You have live ammo and the walls are designed to absorb without allowing the bullets to bounce around the room. Be sure of your targets and always know where your teammates are at all times. Don't get fancy, just move and shoot. If we both engage the same target no big deal as long as we clear the room in allowable time. Understand?"

"What is the allowable time?"

"Now that is the question, isn't it? Only the controllers up in the walkways above us know that and will tell us when finished."

"Okay, then I guess I'm ready. I take it you are the team leader then?"

"Yes, we move, shoot and communicate all at the same time. Multi-tasking the old fashion way."

Dotty drew her pistol, double checked to insure it was ready and positioned it in ready as her other hand reached for the door knob. Megan drew hers and checked it then looked at Janice who was standing behind her ready for targets. Dotty opened the door and moved quickly inside. Dotty was firing as Megan entered and took out an armed target to the left of Dotty and was firing on another as she heard Janice firing behind her as Dotty was taking another target.

As they cleared the room, Janice moved to the next door and took a quick look to see Dotty moving in behind her as Megan moved in behind Dotty. She opened the door and was moving and firing as each woman moved in the room. Megan nearly shot a small child standing on a chair, but held the shot and took the armed, masked man standing behind the child. Dotty called out, Megan, door, and Megan moved to the next door as she dropped her empty magazine and loaded a fresh one. She heard two more magazines hit the floor and paused for a second listening to both women slamming fresh magazines into their weapons. Megan opened the door and moved through it and found no targets. The room was completely empty, so she moved to the next door, looked to see where the other two were and opened the door. She took three targets before she heard the first shot behind her.

They took a total of seven rooms before Dotty opened the door to the hallway and holster her weapon as she stepped through the door. Megan and Janice joined her as Janice began to laugh as Dotty joined her. Megan thought these women were slightly off their rocker but then thought about the last two rooms and had to laugh. Clowns with machine guns!

"Damn Dotty, I haven't had that much fun in ages. Jake would have enjoyed those last two rooms!"

"Janice, he suggested those rooms." Came a male's voice from the overhead walkways.

Dotty looked up and smiled.

"Get you old ass down here Top and meet Miss Wagner."

"I'll be down once I have the final results. Go collect your empty magazines and I'll meet you in the room with your bags."

Fifteen minutes later a gruff looking older gentleman entered the room as the women were sorting out the magazines. He was in civilian clothes and had a neatly trimmed beard. Dotty then Janice hugged him, both planting kisses on his cheeks. They introduced him to Megan.

"Miss Wagner, may I say that whoever taught you to shoot did a fine job of it. I've seen your training records from the Farm but not your service records. Was your father a Marine?"

"No sir, Special Forces. His last assignment was with Delta."

"Horace Wagner?"

"Why yes. Do you know him?"

"Yes, we have shot against each other many times in service matches. He is one puss ugly gentleman to have such a lovely daughter as you. It must be your mother's influence to the gene pool."

Megan laughed at his statement and took an immediate liking to the man. She gave him a quick kiss on his cheek which made him blush then he opened the folder he was carrying. It showed how many rounds each person had fired by room and total rounds fired. It also gave number of hits and misses on each target. Megan had the fewest rounds fired but they were nearly all equal in targets taken with Megan edging Dotty out by only one target with Janice one target behind Dotty.

When Peters left, Dotty just sat in her chair and smiled at Megan as she removed a folder from her range bag. She took a letter from the folder and handed it over to Megan which she recognized it as a copy of the letter she had sent to the Director of Operations. Dotty then pulled an identification wallet from her bag and handed it to Megan. The wallet identified her as Dorothy M. Collins, Assistant Deputy Director of Operations. Director of Planning Analysis.

"Megan, do you still want the answers to the questions you posed in that letter?"

"Yes, I do Ma'am."

"Megan, no need to call me Ma'am. We don't operate that way in the Dungeon. As of right now you work for me. I'll explain what we do when you report for duty next Monday, but I will tell you this. You will be armed at all times. Also, we have a condo for you in McLean so you will have more privacy than in an apartment."

"Thank you Mrs. Collins."

"Dorothy or Dotty in private or in the Dungeon. Janice, when are you heading home?"

"I'm having dinner with Bill and Hanna tonight, then Peters wants me to help him with a group of female Marine Officer Candidates in the morning. Probably have dinner with him tomorrow night then head back home. But I'll let you buy lunch at the Officer's club."

Dotty laughed. "You're on. Let's get this mess cleaned up, I'm starving and eating for two now."

They ate at the Officer's Club and talked about the Funhouse they had just ran through. Janice had taken her wedding rings from the chain around her neck and put them back on her finger as Dotty only wore a simple, gold wedding band. Megan was approached as she was returning from the lady's room by a Marine Major wearing a flight suit, but she was polite in telling the officer she was just passing through and was a guest of a friend today. He watched her as she returned to her table and just watched her as she finished lunch.

Dotty and Janice both commented on how he was looking at her. Megan finally reached into her purse and removed her CIA identification and walked over to him with it in hand. He stood when she approached his table and she carefully opened it between them, so he could see it as she smiled and told him once again she was passing through and to save his energies for someone who could not kill him with her bare hands. She never stopped smiling as she turned back to her table, leaving him standing unsure of what just happened to his hopes of seeing her laid out on his bed.

As they finished lunch, Dotty explained to Megan that Janice was one of the original members of the Dungeon team and had married the first head of the Dungeon and both had retired from government service. Janice would sometimes return as a civilian contractor as would her husband, Doctor Grainger otherwise known as the Gunner. Megan was further advised that she was replacing one of the team members who had been injured in a traffic accident that left them permanently in a wheelchair.

On the way back to the Farm, Janice and Megan talked about many things including what the mission of the Dungeon crew was in plain terms. Janice never mentioned the operation to kidnap Mohammadi or the traitors within the government they helped take down. She never asked Megan about her last assignment or her background other than her college education. Janice did complement her on her language skills and asked her if she spoke any other languages.   Megan told her, and Janice smiled telling her she would be an asset to the Dungeon crew.

After Janice dropped Megan off at her quarters, Megan took a look at her eight-year old Toyota and decided it was time to upgrade her transportation. She knew she had plenty of money in her bank accounts, so she changed her clothing and left the Farm to see about a new vehicle. Megan returned just before the dining hall closed for the evening driving a new, red Tahoe.

When she signed out the next morning, once again she was handed an envelope containing the address and keys to the condo she would occupy while assigned to Langley. Her assignment orders were in a separate envelope. This was Thursday and she had until Monday to report. Megan went to visit her parents at their Spring Lake farm and moved into her condo late Sunday afternoon. She ate Chinese carry-out that evening and decided to fill the fridge Monday after work.

Welcome to the Dungeon

The first day at any new job can be both exciting and disappointing in many ways. For Megan it got interesting before she ever entered the building. She remembered what she needed to get a car into the compound from her first trip to Langley which sped up the entrance process, but she was met before she ever entered the building by Bill Rendell.

Bill stopped her from entering the building with a smile and his identification in hand. He explained he was the Number Two man at Planning Analysis and he was there to insure she was properly checked in without delays. He asked her if she was carrying her sidearm, she told him no, she had left it in her vehicle.

"Miss Wagner, you will be armed portal to portal meaning from the door of the condo to this door behind us. Return to your vehicle and retrieve your sidearm, then we shall proceed with getting you checked in."

Bill watched her walk away thinking about the report he had read on her earlier this morning. Single, unattached with no known affiliations with either sex. He also remembered the report on the warehouse ambush especially her Marine escort's statement on how cool she was described to be when face with overwhelming odds against her. Three dead men attested to her ability to defend herself. Dotty said she never hesitated in the shooting rooms at the fun house as she worked her way through various scenarios. Intelligent, attractive and deadly. A lethal combination.

Once Megan received her new credentials along with her license to carry a firearm, Bill took her up to the Dungeon. As they were going up on the elevator, he told her that their current spaces were four times larger than when they started in a conference room. Entrance was tightly controlled and restricted to a short list beyond those employed there. The door he took her too was only marked 'Office of Planning Analysis' and he had her swipe her identification card at the entry control. The door unlocked, and he opened it then ushered her in.

As soon as the door opened, she heard music. It took her a moment to realize it was Shubert, but she couldn't remember which one it was. She stepped through the door and came face to face with a man sitting behind a desk smiling at her. He only nodded to her and she nodded back. Behind him was a wall that when she followed it to her right there was an opening at the far end. Looking left, the wall ended the same way and there was another man sitting in a chair against the far wall with a magazine in his hands looking at her. It dawned on her these were security personal there to prevent unauthorized individuals from entering further into the office if they had been able to get pass the coded door.

Bill nudged her towards the right and she headed for the entrance into the working area of the room. She turned the corner into the room and paused as she took it all in. She was expecting cubicles but what she saw was a wide-open workspace. Along the wall to her left were computer work stations which she did a quick assessment determining one station per individual. At the far end was a desk which she determined to belong to Dotty with a coffee station on one side and a fridge and small table on the other side.

In the middle of the room was another computer facing the wall to her right which as she moved further into the room was covered with white boards, cork boards and a huge, wall mounted flat screen television. Eight-foot tables were arranged between the computer and the television monitor. Dotty was standing at the end of the tables with six people standing behind her. Dotty pointed a remote to Megan's left and the music ceased.

"Megan, Welcome to the Dungeon. I'll do a quick introduction and let everyone give you a quick background on themselves as time permits. Team, Megan comes to us from Operations where she was a Field Officer in Korea working under a State Department cover. She was wounded in her right thigh during an ambush outside the embassy where a State Department co-worker was critically injured but survived her wounds. I'll not say anymore right now other than Megan cleaned my clock along with Janice's at the Funhouse Thursday. After she gets up to speed with our programs, we'll all take a trip back to the Funhouse and see what Peters can do to confound us."

Dotty then started doing the introductions. Dave was her husband and also head of their security and transportation. Tyler was a small man who came to them from Intelligence. Kathy was a forty something redhead who came to the crew from Communications. Gretchen was a tall blond who was their combination Secretary/IT tech. Ron was a big man on the verge of becoming obese who had come over from Operations. Melvin or Mel was originally not a CIA employee, but was seconded over from the FBI during one operational review to trace the flow of funds on the other side. He stayed as a full time CIA employee working in the Dungeon.

Dotty motioned towards the entrance to her right and Megan noticed both of the men who were sitting on the other side of the wall were standing there. Dotty indicated the taller of the two as William, their primary driver when any of the team has to be transported during the day. Clifton was their security officer for the same reason. They also took part in the analyzing of operations when not required elsewhere. Dotty then turned back to the tables in the middle of the room and pointed to them.

"People this is our mission today. This is Operation Sierra which Dave and Bill will recognize therefore they are exempt except to assist Megan in wandering through our madness."

She opened the larger of the two boxes and removed a thick file.

"This is a previous review of the operation which will stay in my desk until we complete the package here. Dave, Bill help but no sneaky hints on this one, let everyone find the problems themselves. One other thing people, this is the operation that actually caused the formation of the Dungeon. Get to work people."

She took the folder to her desk, opened a drawer and placed it into it then sat down behind her desk to watch the crew start laying out folders on the tables. Bill motioned for Megan to a computer work station where she finally saw her name tacked to the wall above the computer monitor. The name tag was in purple with black lettering. Megan stepped back and noticed each person had a different color as a background. When she looked at Bill he smiled then opened the top right-hand drawer of her desk. It was full of purple dry markers for the white boards and other types of pens all in purple.

"Megan, any notes you make to the white boards or elsewhere will be in purple. This is a method of tracking who does what without signing off or notating each note. It'll make sense over time."

Dave walked up to Megan's station and between him and Bill they explained how they operated and functioned. Megan placed her purse under the desk then walked over to the tables and just stood and watched as the rest of the crew were dissecting the files. Photos were being placed on the cork boards by date/time and from time to time an individual would make a note on the white board. Megan walked over to the photos and studied them one at a time as she worked her way through the drone photos of the target location. She paused at one point then stepped back looking at them again before going back to her work station and took a dry write pen from her desk. She moved to the white board and read the comments already on it before posting a question of where were a couple of photos and why were they missing from the list of photos in the file.

Gretchen walked over to the white board, read the comments then went to the cork boards on the other side on the large monitor. She did a quick review of the information posted there, tapped one with her pen then returned to notate Megan's question about the photo's being listed as duplicates. Megan stood looking at the photos after she had read Gretchen's note and checking the photo listing. She just stood looking at the photos and was not aware she was shaking her head when Dave softly spoke behind her.

"What's the problem Megan?"

"This is wrong. Something is missing, and I'll bet a dinner it's in the missing photos."

"Alright, how would you correct the problem?"

"Not sure since the dates are over eight years ago, but I'd want to know if the missing photos still exist before attempting to find another avenue to the answer if one even exists."

"Fine, now if you have a question you need an immediate answer to, speak up. Posting to the board is great but only as long as it does not slow down the process. Understand?"

Megan turned to look up at him then back to the chaos around her.

"How can I find out if the missing photos listed as duplicates still exist?"

Mel looked at her and smiled before he called out to Clifton.

"Megan write down the data from the photos at the bottom for both photos on the board and ask for the missing photo between them. Clifton will act as our courier and try to recover them from the archives."

Megan looked back to see Clifton standing inside the room waiting. She took a pad from the table along with a pen and wrote the sequence data from the photos as Mel had indicted and walked to Clifton and handed it to him. She explained what she needed, and he just nodded and left on his mission. Megan then went to the corkboard and read the actual operation profile then the after-action report. She stood a long time looking at the report on the board and Dave noticed she seemed lost.

"Megan, are you alright?"

"Do we have a list of the Rangers killed in action?"

"No, we only see the names of lost Field Officers, never the names of any service members killed during one of our missions."

Megan turned to look at Dotty behind her desk watching them.

"Dotty, can we get a list of the Rangers killed in action?"

Everyone stopped what they were doing waiting for Dotty to answer. Dotty looked at Megan and could not read the look on her face.

"Gretchen?"

"I'm on it Dotty. Megan this could take some time."

"I understand, thank you."

Megan picked up a notepad and started making notes on it as she waited for Gretchen to deal with her request. She had a page and a half of double space notes when Gretchen walked over to her and hand her a printout. Megan thanked her and studied the list of killed and wounded. She looked at the list a long time before a hand carefully pulled it from her grasp. She looked at the owner of the hand and Dotty was standing beside her. It was then she noticed that once again the commotion in the room had ceased as everyone was looking at her.

"Alright Megan, you have seen the list. Now explain why you wanted it."

"Sergeant First Class Michael Davenport."

"Okay, what about him?"

"He was my God-Father. The Army reported him killed in a training accident. A helicopter crash, but my Father always seemed to know differently. His daughter, Marie never questioned the Purple Heart she received on his behalf after the funeral. A closed casket funeral."

"Megan, you can never speak to anyone outside this room about how he died. Besides being classified information, it will not do anyone any good. It will only bring back bad memories."

"Yes Dotty I understand. I wish I had never asked for the information now."

"Megan, understand this. We must ask hard questions in this room. Even questions with answers that can be painful. We deal with failed operations in this room and that usually means people died during those operations. The very first operation we examined was one where Janice was wounded and men in her operational team were killed. Janice blamed herself for the failure of that mission as did the powers to be, but the team, well mostly the Gunner, proved she was innocent of any blame."

Dotty gave it a moment for her words to sink in.

"But we are not here to place blame or prove innocence; we are here to find the errors in intelligence or planning so they can be corrected in the future. What we are doing here today is purely a training exercise. The errors previously discovered in this operation have been corrected. Now, do you wish to be excluded from this exercise or stay with it?"

"I'll stay. Sorry, I never should have asked for that list."

"You're wrong there. Not asking for any type of information can lead to deadly consequences. Just make sure your reasons are not personal in nature but apply to the operation."

"How could you be sure my question was not personal when you approved my request?"

"Megan my first husband was an Army officer, a helicopter pilot killed in action in Iraq. I have your personal records in my desk and know what your father did in the Army. It was a risk approving your request, but it was one that I felt was justified in bringing you into the fold. Once more, do you wish to continue with this operation?"

"Yes Dotty, I do. Thank you."

"Good, now get back to work because if you will notice, no one is working because they are waiting for one of us to smack the other one."

Megan laughed then went back to the photos as the crew got back to work. Notepad in hand, Megan moved from board to board looking for answers. If she could not find an answer to a question on her pad, she wrote it on the white board then moved on to the next question. If she found the answer, she notated it on her pad and once again moved to the next question. Tyler asked her once if she needed any help finding something which she answered no, but if she did she'd let him know.

She was reading a report pinned to the boards when she heard her name softly spoken beside her. Clifton was standing there, holding a large envelope out to her. She smiled at him, took the envelope and told him thanks for his efforts. He just nodded and returned to his station outside the room. Megan pulled the photos from the envelope, checked the sequencing numbers and date/time before pinning them to the boards so they were positioned in their proper spot. It only took her a couple minutes before she recognized what was missing from the other photos.

Instead of notifying any of the other personal about her find, she went to her work station, turned on her computer and followed the access procedure on the card taped to the bottom of the monitor. She went to Google Earth and imputed the coordinates of the campsite in the photos and waited for Goggle to catch up. When the location came up, she noticed the date on the satellite view was over a week old but that did not matter at this time. She zoomed in on the photo until she had the view which confirmed what she suspected. Megan printed the photo and then went into the Google menu and asked for the same location on the date of the rescue mission. It gave her a pop-up notice that the photos could not be found.

Megan took the photo to the boards and double checked the intelligence report giving the estimate of personal in the camp before she pinned the Goggle photo to the boards. She looked around the room to see what Tyler was doing before calling him over to the photos.

"Tyler, this is the missing photo shown as a duplicate. Here is a photo from Goggle Earth taken a week ago. What do you see?"

Tyler studied the photos for several minutes often standing real close to the boards. He went to his desk and retrieved a magnifying glass and continued his exam until he stepped back, shaking his head. He had a disgusted look on his face as he spoke to Megan.

"Megan, unless I am grossly mistaken, those Rangers were badly outnumbered when they hit that camp. That changes the equation but have you asked yourself how the bad guys reacted so quickly to the raid at that time of night?"

"I have and I seriously doubt the Rangers did something stupid alerting those in the camp of their presence as they moved on it."

"This smells of someone having advanced notice of the raid and they were ready for it."

"I agree."

Tyler raised his voice. "Hey people, Megan has found something that everyone needs to see."

Everyone moved to Megan and she found herself the center of attention which actually made her uncomfortable. No one spoke as Megan collected herself, but Tyler seemed to notice she was unsure how to frame her comments and spoke for her.

"People, Megan has figured out why the Rangers were outgunned. The intelligence package was grossly flawed. They never had a chance, but she also feels the other side had prior notice of the raid. Right, Megan?"

"Yes Tyler, if you examine the missing photos, they show a dark shadow on both sides of the camp. Shadows in the form of structures. I pulled up a recent Goggle Earth photo of the area and the remains of those structures can be seen even after all these years. Please, everyone take a look to be sure."

"Megan, advanced notice would mean someone within the system betrayed the Rangers. Can we be sure they did not blow the approach?" Melvin inquired.

"Melvin, I am an Army brat. My father is Special Forces and I am confident in stating they don't make those kinds of mistakes. If something had happened to alert the camp, they never would have attacked as they did based on the After-Action reports. They would have adjusted their method of advance before continuing with the operation. I know that is a biased statement on my part, but it is based on firsthand knowledge of living with those kinds of men for most of my life."

"She's right Melvin." Bill spoke up. "Remember I was a Ranger and we always had a back-up plan in case of changes on the target."

"Alright people, examine the photos again and let's see if anyone wishes to disagree with what Megan and Tyler have determined." Dave instructed.

Everyone examined the photos and came up with the same conclusion concerning the Rangers being outnumbered. But it was Ron who asked the one question no one had asked yet.

"I wonder how many of the bad guys were in that camp."

"I can answer that." Dotty spoke up as she was standing behind the group. "I think we can safely assume that not only was the intelligence package flawed but it is highly possible of advance warning of the raid. Any one disagree with that assumption?"

No one spoke up even though they knew it was allowed to disagree with the boss.

"Clear the boards and I'll let Dave post the data in the folder in my desk."

Megan was unsure how to proceed with the repacking of the files but helped as she could. At some time during the repacking, everyone congratulated her on her discovery which seemed to lighten her up some knowing how her God-Father had actually died. Inside she wanted to go out and find the bastards who had caused his death, especially the individual who had warned the guerillas of the raid.

Dave waited until a full set of boards were cleared before he began to post the next set of photos and reports. Megan was tempted to start reading the information but held off until Dave finished and Dotty gave the go ahead. When the crew was told to examine the next set of data, Megan held back, allowing the others to go first. She heard several people make comments, mostly in the nature of 'Sweet Jesus' or 'Damn' as they read the reports and reviewed the photos.

Any thoughts of hunting down the guerillas ended as she read the reports. The final after action report amazed her in that six men went into the guerilla camp and wiped out ninety-three guerillas without suffering a single injury and not only recovered the kidnapped CIA Field Officer but a French engineer who was assumed dead. Megan was looking at the photos taken a day later of the bodies lying on the bunks, all shot in the head when a female voice asked the question going through her mind.

"Was this one of our Special Ops teams that did this?"

Suddenly a photo was flashed upon the big screen between the boards. In it was a photo of a Marine Officer in his dress blues and a beautiful woman in a matching gown. It only took Megan a second to recognize Janice in the photo but could tell from the others comments they knew the Marine.

"Megan, that is a photo of Gunner Grainger who was the first director of this group. He privately ran a black ops team, off the books of the government and planned then executed the operation. Dave, Bill and I have met the entire team later on during the final phase of determining who informed on the Rangers. That situation has been resolved and that is all any of us familiar with it can say. In fact, much of what we discovered here and even planned here is still a current operation."

"Thank you, Dotty."

"Now clean up this mess, we have another training package to deal with today."

The week went by with the crew doing a total of three training exercises as Megan became a solid member of the crew. She noticed that several members would pair up, but she stayed apart from pairing up, but did join with others for bits and pieces of a problem. When she was not working on a training problem, she was at her computer researching the gang in Japan that had attacked her, and any information she could find about the attack on her and Linda in Seoul. Megan kept hitting blocks within the CIA system during this research due to security levels above her own. Dotty came by her station and told her to relax; they'd get to her situation as soon as she was fully into the fold and understood how the Dungeon worked.

The next two weeks went by quickly as they went through exercise after exercise with Megan learning the strengths and weaknesses of each of the team members. She also discovered her own weaknesses which left her with a profound sense of inadequacy for the first time in her life. Megan worked hard at removing her weaknesses to the point Kathy pulled her aside and told her to slow down and relax. No one was perfect, and it was a team effort not an individual effort. This was later echoed by Melvin after she got angry at herself for making what she considered a stupid mistake. Megan found the team was working to help her through the problems and she was fighting them as she tried to correct her mistakes. She was no longer an independent operator, but part of a team.

Five weeks after Megan reported to the Dungeon, she walked in to see a photo up on the large monitor that shocked her. It was a photo of her in a bloody dress holding up Conley with bodies lying about her. Both faces had been blurred out, but she did not need to see her face to know that was her. Dotty captured her before she could speak and just linked arms with her as she took her to her work station before speaking to the crew who were looking at the photo.

"Alright people listen up. What we have here is the attempted murder of a State Department employee in Japan. The female is that employee, and the male is her Marine escort. The reports are in the box on the table. You will notice the names of the female and male have been redacted, but that is not a problem. What we need to consider here is why they were attacked in the first place. What situation created the necessity to end their lives? Also note that their Japanese driver was murdered before they came after the pair. Let's find some answers folks."

Dotty turned to Megan and spoke to her in a low voice.

"Megan, you can stay on the edge of this but watch your comments. Do not allow anyone here to know that is you in the photo. That information will come to surface soon enough, but right now we can see what the others can discover."

"Alright Dotty, I'll play the game."

Ten minutes after the crew got the go on this problem, Megan heard Ron comment about the female that had killed three men in quick order. Then he asked the question that suddenly popped into everyone's mind.

"Dotty, are we sure she is State Department? Three men in hand to hand combat. She sounds more like a highly trained CIA Field Officer."

44

Suddenly every person turned to look at Megan knowing she had come to them from Operations, and had been in Korea. She looked at Dotty who gave her a nod yes.

'Yes Ron, she is a highly trained Field Officer. She has been taught GoJuRu Karate since she was old enough to walk by her uncle who has a Dojo on Okinawa, and her Special Forces father, who is also a Second Degree Black Belt. But take note that the Marine Lance Corporal with her killed two men, and put one out of action also. No, she does not know why she was attacked but she has several ideas. None of which she will share with you until you have taken this as far as humanly possible."

No one spoke as they suddenly went to work on the problem before them. Find the reason or reasons Megan and the Marine were attacked. Mel divided the white boards into two groups. What they know and what they suspect. Soon the boards were being notated on both sides as theories were developed or agreed with. By the end of the day, nothing was determined with more questions than answers. Megan had stayed out of the way watching the crew work, and before she left for the day she notated a couple of the theories as ones she also held.

The next morning the photo of the two assassins lying beside their crashed cab was on the monitor. William and Clifton had been included in this problem and after reading the report on the shooting, William asked Megan about her leg. Megan said it was fully functional and pulled up her skirt to show the slight scar of her wound. No other comments were made as once more they audited the reports and made changes to the white boards.

Megan was finally able to review the photos of the crime scene and posted a question of her own about if these were the complete set of photos of the crime scene. Soon Gretchen notated to Megan's question that a request had been made to the embassy in Japan to insure all photos taken by both U.S. sources and the Japanese were available for review.

It was close to the end of the day when Megan posted another question. Where and what was the status of Lance

Corporal Conley. Dotty posted a note that a request had been made to Headquarters Marine Corps concerning his status. Once more there were more questions than answers when the day ended. Megan was becoming frustrated at the fact that even with the resources of the CIA, they could not seem to answer the simplest of questions.

On Thursday, Dotty told the crew they were taking a road trip to Quantico and play in the fun house. The back ground on the gang members at the warehouse and that of Megan's ambushers was slowly coming into focus. The shooters had no gang allegiance, but it was discovered they had a large amount of cash in American dollars in their possession at their time of death. A question was posed whether they were paid to kill Megan and why she to be killed was still another question needing to be answered.

A Marine & A Motel Room

Megan ran the Funhouse partnered with Dave and Bill as the first team through the scenarios. She had to admit they were good but not as good as Dotty and Janice. Later she ran through another set of rooms with Kathy and Ron. Ron surprised her because as large as he was, he was light on his feet and was on par with either Bill or Dave. Kathy needed more range time and a steady hand to help her improve her abilities, but she was giving it all she had from the first door.

The day was going quick with the Funhouse crew resetting each room once the tactical team had left it for the next room. Megan quickly broke her Sig down, brushed the carbon off the frame and slide and ran an oily swab down the barrel after her last run, then reloaded her magazines. She was talking to Kathy about how to handle the rooms when Dotty called out to her.

"Megan, room one! They are waiting on you!"

Megan took off at a run and as she turned the hallway corner to the door for room one, she saw a man's back as he opened the door and entered followed my Master Sergeant Peters who looked at her before entering the room. She entered behind them as the shooting stopped and heard Peters call out to her to take the door. She passed by the two men, took the door and once more it was leap frog from room to room without Megan ever getting a clear view of the other man teamed up with her and Peters.

She took the door to room five and saw it was empty. As she started moving towards the next door, she heard Peters call out cease fire. Megan was beginning to feel tired from the stress of working the rooms especially having to run to the start and not getting there on time. She holstered her Sig and turned to look at Peters as the other man entered the room. It took a second to recognize who this man was as he walked up to her with a smile on his face and offered his hand.

"Megan Wagner, it is a pleasure to meet you. My name is Jake Grainger. Janice said you were damn good and I have to say she was not lying. Now I'm not going to waste your time or the time the others need in this place, so as I understand it, you are asking questions that no one seems to have the answers too."

"Yes Sir, I am. Is that wrong of me?"

"No, but you need to fix the problem with your impatience concerning this matter. It does nothing more than lead you into making mistakes that are often fatal. Nature sets the course of the universe and any attempt to rush nature gains nothing but heartache."

"I'm not sure what that means but I accept my own faults. What do I do now?"

Jake reached into his pants pocket and removed a memory stick and handed it to her.

"This is a gift, but additional information comes with a price. I understand that you are aware I ran a black ops organization before coming to the CIA to start the Department of Planning Analysis. I used them to also stop a traitor from taking over the CIA and the country. Some of the information you have been asking for is on that stick, as is a manner of contacting those who can get you more answers. Do not question who these people are behind the scenes and at some point, they may ask for your help in doing something for this country. I retired as did my team, but you can find a list buried deep inside that stick of people who can and will help if need be."

Megan looked at the memory stick in her hand, then back up at Jake.

"Who asked you to obtain this information on the stick?"

"No one asked me for anything except to insure you receive that stick. I'm just the messenger today."

"Am I being recruited?"

"That is a question only you can answer. Today I am only the messenger. When we exit this room, I'm heading for the NCO Club and have a drink with an old friend, then home to build my son a tree house. Megan, you have great potential but learn to be patient before you become one needing major medical to repair your impatience."

He walked pass her and exited with Peters following behind him. Megan heard shooting as she headed for the door and had three range personnel entering with target dummies to prepare the room for the next shooting team. She pocketed the memory stick and headed down the hallway to the ready room. She walked up to Dotty and whispered in her ear.

"Did you arrange that meeting with the Gunner?"

"No, in fact I didn't know the Gunner was even here until I saw him in the hallway with Peters. Keep whatever he said to you to yourself. What I do not know I cannot be held accountable for and somewhat knowing the Gunner's previous life, I really do not want to know what happened here today. Do we understand each other?"

"Completely. He did tell me to curb my impatience. Did you say anything to him?"

"No Megan, but it does not surprise me that he knows. No more than it would surprise me to find out one or more people working in the Dungeon is keeping him appraised of what goes on in there. I owe him more than I could ever repay him, but even I have my limits of what I will tolerate, even for him."

"I understand Dotty."

"I don't think so Megan, but you will in time."

Dotty left Megan wondering what was happening in her life that put her into this situation with a boss who just left her hanging in the wind unsure of what to do, but telling her to be careful in whatever she did.

Megan ran one last set of rooms this time using Dotty's Walther. She liked it but preferred her Sig. The trip back to Langley was full of the others talking about how they did in each set of rooms, with Ron and others commenting on how well Megan shot and moved from one room to another. Before Dotty kicked them loose for the weekend, she told them that starting Monday they would hit the exercise equipment twice a week, on Tuesday and Thursday's and a minimum of one-hour range time on Wednesday's. Kathy approached Megan and asked her to help her improve her shooting abilities which Megan told her she would be happy too.

When Megan got home, she cleaned her Sig and checked her magazines for dents as they dropped to the floor then insured they were all loaded before putting them back in the range bag. She showered before fixing something to eat then sat down at her computer and stared at the memory stick on the desk in front of her. She disconnected the fire wire from the back of her computer and inserted the memory stick in a USB port once the computer was up and running. There were twelve gigabits of data on the stick and she spent the entire weekend reading the information on it. She never opened the last folder on the stick as it was marked "In Case of Future Need" which was what she considered to be the price of more information.

When Megan reported to work on Monday, she brought with her nearly one hundred pages of information she had printed off the memory stick. On her desk she found a folder containing a copy of the service records of James Lynn Conley. James had recently been promoted to Corporal and was assigned to Headquarters Company, Headquarters Battalion, Second Marine Division at Camp Lejeune. The commendation she had written was in his records along with a Letter of Meritorious Mast, a Marine's version of a Letter of Commendation was also there concerning his actions in the warehouse.

Megan was studying James' photo when Dotty came up to her station and leaned over to also look at his photo.

"Not a bad looking young man your Marine."

"He's not my Marine, but he stood fast when trouble occurred instead of finding a way out of harm's way. Daddy always said Marines tend to hold what they have when men with good sense looked for a way out of trouble. And yes, he is not all that bad looking a man. What can I do for you Dotty?"

"I understand you may have something for me. Something I'm not supposed to have but need to help solve the problem of someone trying to kill you."

"Did someone call you?"

"No, but knowing the Gunner, he probably gave you something I am not to know about, but that is standard operating procedure for him. You would be amazed at the amount of data he brought into the group in those early days. Some was even hand carried and delivered to him here. Drove the Director and the Deputy Directors crazy for a time, but they were smart enough not to interfere with the flow of information."

Megan picked up the shoulder bag she had brought in today and took out a thick stack of papers held together with a large metal spring clip and handed they to Dotty. Dotty looked at them then smiled.

"Jake had a saying. Ask me no questions and I'll tell you no lies. So, I won't ask how or where you got this information and you will not have to lie to me about that situation."

Dotty walked away from Megan towards her desk and Megan realized that a certain level of duplicity had taken place which put her in not only the driver's seat, but the hot seat if things went wrong. She suddenly realized her impatience in nearly demanding answers had driven her into this situation. She was not obligated to anyone for this data but if she pushed any more buttons, she would be, and she had no idea what the cost would be to obtain it.

Megan took another long look at James' photo, and then set his records aside for the time being. Another time or place under the right conditions, a man like James might have been fun to know. But the information she had received answered a lot of questions concerning the people she had killed, but not why she had to kill them. What she had yet to tell anyone was that day was beginning to invade her dreams at night. It scared her that she was aware she was starting to feel the effects of PTSD as she was becoming obsessed with finding the answers to her questions.

Dotty gave the crew the reports that Megan had given her, and they took them apart page by page and put the information on the boards. They had clear ideas of who the people were and their normal business dealings. The Japanese police had determined that Megan had interrupted a hijacking situation and that was the reason for them trying to kill her and Conley. But this did not fit these peoples modus operandi. They were missing something, something that they just could not lay a finger on. Megan looked over at Conley's records and wondered if he had the answer, even if he did not know he had it.

Megan knew that several people had to have seen her pass the stack of papers they were taking apart to Dotty but never commented on where or how the information was obtained. Megan just sat back and let the crew work the information, clearing questions and posting new questions for others to answer. But the final analysis was they still did not have a clear picture of what they had ran into causing the death of five gang members and the incarceration of a sixth.

The information of the failed assassination was even more puzzling in that the two men were small time hoods who had no record of violent crime, and both men had ten thousand U.S. Dollars in their possession at the time of their death. Kathy posted a notation; 'Follow the Money' and Mel went to work trying to find the source of the money.

Megan fought the urge to be impulsive for two days until she finally went to Dotty with an idea. She wanted to know what

Conley remembered about the warehouse. Did he see something she missed? Something that did not seem important to either of them at the time, but was important to the people that tried to kill them. Dotty called Peters and asked him to make a couple inquiries then get back to her as soon as possible. Within an hour Dotty had the answers she needed and gave Megan the go ahead to contact Conley face to face. Dotty was still not sure about bringing Conley to the Dungeon to view the photos they had received on Tuesday, but held that in reserve if Megan was able to get the answers to several of the questions no one in the Dungeon had been able to answer.

On Friday morning, Megan drove down to Jacksonville, North Carolina and took a room at Motel Six so she could change before meeting James at his barracks. Megan decided to have some fun today at James expense but at the same time giving him a reputation he did not deserve with his barracks mates. She dressed in a form fitting little black dress which showed just the right amount of cleavage, black lace thigh high stocking which rose three inches above the inside of her dress hem and calf high black patent leather boots with three-inch heels.

Since leaving the farm, she had let her hair grow and it now reached nearly eight inches below her shoulders. She was only going to brush it out and let it flow over her shoulders giving her a more seductive appearance. Over her dress she was wearing a black Matador jacket with three-quarter length sleeves. Megan had learned to sew before she was ten and had modified this jacket to hold a Sig P238 inside the front left of the jacket and a ceramic knife with five-inch blade in the left inside of the jacket. Both were within easy reach and pull if needed.

A light makeup around her dark eyes and rose lipstick finished her off. Fake diamond ear studs would be the only jewelry today. Megan was grateful for her mother's genes as she had a clear complexion mixed with her father's skin tone. Before she left her room, she laid out jeans, a pull over sweater and everything she might need in case of a hurry to counteract a tactical problem. Ever since she left McLean Virginia, she had the feeling she was being followed, but could never pin down a specific vehicle following her as she stopped for gas or other needs.

Dotty had called the Camp Lejeune Provost Marshall's Office as Megan drove down and advise them of her arrival later in the day, so she would not be delayed entering the Marine Base. She showed her CIA Identification at the Main Gate and was only delayed the time it took to check the posted notice against her ID. Megan had a map of the base with Jeff's Headquarters Company Barracks marked on it and arrived just as the Company was falling into their final formation of the day. She parked away from the formation to their right, exited her Tahoe and walked down the sidewalk to a point anyone in formation could see her, but not so close as to cause a problem. Megan knew how she looked dressed as she was, and she was going to take full advantage of it.

It was not long before the troops began to notice her as their First Sergeant read off different notices to the Marines in formation. Megan was familiar with the process as she had stood near formations her father had stood growing up in the Army. The Company Commander and Company Executive Officer were standing on the sidewalk waiting their turn when they noticed the Marines starting to steal glances in her direction. The Commander leaned over to the Exec and spoke to him. The Exec nodded and came down to where she was standing.

"Can I help you Ma'am?" His tone was soft and polite.

Megan looked at him thinking if he was single, he must have a long string of broken hearts in his wake. She smiled at him.

"Lieutenant, I am waiting to see an old friend once formation is over."

"Who might that be Ma'am?"

"Corporal James Conley. We knew each other in Japan."

"May I see some identification please?"

"Certainly Lieutenant."

Megan reached into her right inside pocket, careful not to expose the stiletto concealed there and took out her CIA Identification and handed it to the Lieutenant.

"Lieutenant, I hope you keep that piece of information between us. It would do no good for the troops to know Corporal Conley has a friend in the spook palace."

He laughed then handed her identification back to her.

"No, no it would not and yes, I'll keep it between us. Now having seen Corporal Conley's records, I seem to remember a commendation from a State Department employee which I believe has your name on it. Am I wrong?"

"No Lieutenant, you are not. Foreign governments do not like spooks in their countries but tend to ignore State Department personal unless they cause problems or trouble."

"I understand. We Marines often have that problem. Formation should be over in about five minutes so if you will wait here, I'll see that Corporal Conley knows that you are here to see him."

He gave her a salute then walked back to the Company Commander and whispered in his ear. The Captain looked at Megan, then leaned back to the Lieutenant and spoke to him. When the First Sergeant finished his duties, he called the formation to attention and turned to the officers. The Company Commander moved to accept the reins of Command and spoke to the men about the previous weeks training and what to expect on Monday. Just before he released the Company he announced that Corporal Conley had a visitor, but did not mention she was standing on the sidewalk. He dismissed the Company and the Platoon Leaders followed suit.

Conley came out of the crowd of Marines that seemed to linger, looking at Megan standing with her ankles crossed and a smile on her face. She heard several men comment to Conley that he was a lucky SOB as he walked up to her and stopped just inside arms reach. Megan stepped forward and hugged him as she planted a kiss on his cheek. He reacted accordingly and hugged her back but stopped short of leaving a kiss on her cheek. Megan released him and stepped back.

"James, it is good to see you. How bad were you hurt?"

"It looked worse than it was. Thanks for the letter of commendation although I only did my duty the best I could. Hell Megan, you did more than I did and took care of me after I was injured."

"You had my back James and a letter of commendation was the most I could do. I'm an Army brat and I've heard awards read for a Bronze Star awarded for less, so let's call it even and never address it again."

"You're on, but now tell me why you are here. I'm a bit suspicious especially the way you are dressed."

Megan laughed.

"James, I would bet your macho points just jumped to the top of the roster which will cause you no end of grief over the next weeks. But I'm here to interview you about the attack in the warehouse. I've read your statement, but there are still several unanswered questions why they attacked us."

"Interview me? Who are you Megan? The way you dealt with those men speaks to me that you are not State Department."

"James, I'm a CIA Field Officer. I was undercover while in Korea and Japan. I can show you my true identification, but I'd prefer not too out in the open this way. I did show them to your Exec earlier but showing them to you can cause questions considering the number of men still watching us. Now I'm going to give you a kiss then you are going to take me to your mess hall and buy me dinner. It has been years since I have eaten in a mess hall and I think I'd like to try yours out."

Megan stepped forward, wrapped her arms around his neck and gave him a soft kiss which he returned as he wrapped his arms around her waist and held her until she broke the kiss. She stepped back and looked at him thinking another time or place, but this was business.

"Megan, what are you carrying inside your jacket?"

"Do you really need to ask?"

"Damn, you are serious. Alright, dinner is on me and we have a damn good mess hall."

He offered her his left arm which she accepted, and they walked to the mess hall with several wolf whistles following them. She told him to find a quiet corner if possible and they'd talk if possible. At the table she sat close to him where she could watch the traffic in the mess hall as she asked him questions about the attack on them. Megan noticed that nearly all the female Marines passing through the mess hall were giving them a good look which made Megan smile inside knowing soon he would have a lot of attention from that quarter. It was one of the reasons she dressed as she had because if she could not get him a medal for his actions, maybe she could assist in getting him laid.

Just as they were finishing chow, Megan mentioned the attempt on her in Seoul which caused James to set back from her and his disposition changed.

"Megan, I was told the men we killed were trying to hijack that shipment of grain seed, but six men to steal thirty tons of grain? They needed trucks and fork lifts to do that and there were none around. So why were those men behind the third stack? Before you answer, there was an attempt on my life while in the Japanese hospital. Only an observant security guard prevented me from getting a syringe full of poison. Megan none of this makes sense."

"James, do you have any duties this weekend?"

"No, I'm off this weekend. Why?"

"You're coming with me tonight. Back to my motel room so we can talk in private more about this."

"Alright, but I have to change into civvies before we go."

They took their dishes to the scullery and walked back to his barracks. Megan had a thought and took him to her Tahoe, removed a high-density flashlight from the console and asked him to examine the underneath of her vehicle. About halfway up the passenger side he found an odd-looking device with a wire hanging from it. She asked him to describe it then told him to leave it alone for now. While he was in the barracks changing, she took two range bags from the back of the Tahoe and placed them in the front of the vehicle.

As she waited on Conley, she sent a text to Dotty. "Attempt made to kill Conley in Japan. He has questions we have not considered. Taking him to motel to further question him. Have found tracking device on Tahoe. Still intact. Will advise if help needed."

James was getting settled into the passenger seat when Dotty's reply arrived.

"Use your best judgement. Will advise Security of possible need at your location. Will advise Lejeune PM of same. Stay loose and be careful."

Megan sent the motel information back to Dotty then pointed out the range bag to Jeff and told him to lock and load. The bag contained a civilian version of the M9 Beretta with seven magazines already loaded. James inserted a magazine and locked and loaded the pistol. After he had safed the weapon, he just looked at Megan as she drove through the base to the front gate.

"Megan, I hope you have a plan that you wish to share with me."

"James, I've notified my boss about the situation and she has a Security detail standing by and is going to alert the Provost Marshall's office of a possible need to assist. See if you can get that shoulder holster on and adjusted so you can carry the Beretta."

"I'm not licensed to carry a firearm in public."

"I'll cover that with my credentials. Just get it done before we get off base please."

It was awkward for James to get the holster on and adjust in the front seat of the Tahoe, but he worked quickly and was back in his jacket before they hit the main gate. He had two extra magazines in his jacket pockets and just waited for further instructions. Megan told him to watch for a vehicle that would appear every time they made a stop since she was planning ahead to give anyone tracking them a chance to expose themselves.

She pulled into the first convenience store outside the base directly at the door where the lights were brightest and gave James several twenty-dollar bills and told him to get a six pack of beer and some snacks. Her next stop was a liquor store where James bought a bottle of champagne. Once James was back in the Tahoe, he told Megan there was a car across the street that was also parked the same way at the convenience store. Megan backed out of the parking space in a manner which would require her to drive past the parked car and took a quick look at it. She wasn't sure but thought the front license plate was from Maryland. She watched her rear mirrors, noticing the car pulled out onto the street behind them.

Megan sent a text to Dotty as she drove. "Tail spotted, enroute to motel. Confirm."

Dotty replied moments later advising her that a Security team was on its way by helicopter.

Megan was unsure if she took a circular route to the motel if it might spook the people tailing them, so she took the most direct route possible. As she pulled into the motel's parking lot she watched as the tail quickly pulled into the strip mall across the street and pulled into a place facing the street turning their headlights out even before they parked. Megan quickly told James to make it look like they were going to have a sweaty night before they entered the room so those following them would think they had not been spotted.

At the door, James pulled Megan close, grabbed her by the ass and kissed her. She played the part hiking a leg up beside him before moving apart so she could open the room door. Once inside and the door closed James apologized for getting so personal and groping her as he had. Megan told him not to worry but keep a watch out the blinds to see if they did anything as she changed.

Megan removed the Sig and stiletto along with her CIA identification from the jacket, placing them on the room's desk then tossing it to the side as she began to strip. Boots and dress were quickly removed and tossed to the side with the jacket. James took a quick look to see her standing wearing only a matching set of black underwear and her thigh high stockings as she first pulled the sweater on then grabbed her jeans. James had to force himself to look out the window instead of admiring Megan's body. She pulled on her field boots and zipped up the sides, pulled her Sig P250 from her purse and shoved it into her holster then picked up her cell phone and put it in her back pocket.

Once dressed Megan stripped the bed of all its linen then told James to help her. They stood the mattress up in front of the window then turned off the room lights. Megan grabbed a couple of bottles of water she already had in the room along with the bag of Doritos and sat down on the floor with her back against the mattress. James took the hint and sat down beside her. Megan opened the Doritos and sat the bag between them.

"Megan, what are you thinking?"

"I'm thinking that if I was going to kill an individual that had entered a motel room with one of the opposite sex, I'd wait until they were hot and sweaty to make the hit. I'd say fifteen minutes after the lights went out. What do you think?"

"Fifteen minutes sounds about right. But myself, forty-five minutes would be closer to right with a woman like you. Time to enjoy the company before enjoying the company."

Megan laughed.

Across the street the two men had the same idea. The passenger had exited the car and had gone to the back to build a Molotov cocktail to toss through the motel room's window after the driver had shot it out. When the driver started their stolen car, he thought to himself they should have stolen a different car that didn't have a squealing serpentine belt under the hood.

Megan was sitting there with her eyes closed listening for anything out of the normal. She heard the squeal of the belt as the car entered the motel's parking lot and tapped James on the leg. James looked up to make sure the door was locked, and the safety bar was in place as he drew the Beretta. They both heard the car stop but the motor never stopped running as indicated by the slight squealing of the belt.

The two men exited the car with the driver carrying an AK-47 with two magazines taped together. The passenger had a Glock in the front of his pants and the Molotov cocktail he had constructed across the street. The driver stepped up on the sidewalk between the window and Megan's Tahoe, then opened fire on the window at an angle if he figured right would kill anyone lying where he estimated the bed to be in the motel room. He emptied the magazine, changed to the full one and started firing again as his partner lit the Molotov cocktail.

Megan and James were down low as the bullets tore through the mattress and chewed up the box springs and opposite wall. They heard the pause between changing magazines then heard a voice telling the shooter to move out of the way. Outside the man with the Molotov threw it at the window as hard as he could not realizing he may have been able to throw it through the blinds but not a mattress. The bottle hit the mattress and bounced back at the men barely missing the man who had thrown it, but hit the bumper of the Tahoe exploding causing both men to be doused by flaming gasoline setting them on fire.

As soon as the screams of the men were heard inside, James was moving, unlocking the door then waited as Megan slid along the floor so she had a clear field of vision once the door was opened. Since the door had an automatic closure, James pointed at it with his Beretta and Megan nodded her understanding. She lowered her Sig so he could cross her field of fire without risk as he opened the door. All that Megan saw when the door opened was the legs of a man on fire lying on the sidewalk. James stepped to the edge of the door and looked down the sidewalk then motioned to Megan to exit the room. She moved quickly jumping over the burning legs in front of the door then James followed her out into the parking lot to see if any others were present to cause them harm.

James turned off the engine of the car and put the keys in his pocket. Megan pulled her cell phone out and instead of texting Dotty she placed a call. Dotty answered on the first tone.

"Dotty, two men attempted hit on us at the motel. Both are dead by their own hands in a failed attempt to use a Molotov cocktail. We are alright and have done a quick check of the area. Awaiting advice or orders."

"Hold what you have, and I'll call the MP's to provide help."

Dotty hung up on Megan and made her calls. Megan went back to the sidewalk in time to see a man in his underwear with a fire extinguisher put out the fire in the window, then the front of her Tahoe before using the last of his fire extinguisher on the bodies on the sidewalk. He just sat the extinguisher down then walked back to his room five doors down to get dressed. Megan noticed the vehicle in front of his room was a construction vehicle and there was an empty bracket for a fire extinguisher just behind the driver's door. James walked up beside Megan and stood with his back to her looking out over the parking lot as the hotel's fire alarm was sounding.

"Problem Megan?"

"Yeah, I've only made three payments on my truck and now look at it."

James looked over at the front of the Tahoe and shook his head.

"Megan, go get packed up and ready to roll if need be, I've got this out here. Sirens are coming, and you still need to cover my ass about having this Beretta."

She looked at James, then went back into the smoke-filled room. The lights still worked, and she quickly gathered up her things and tossed them into her bags. She brought them out to the sidewalk as the first fire truck arrived followed by a police car. James had the Beretta down at his side as Megan stepped out in front of him with her identification held high for the police officers to see. He only holstered the Beretta when she ordered him to.

Soon the parking lot filled with police cars creating a minor traffic jam until the Police Lieutenant on duty sent all but three cars back on patrol. Military Police showed up and stood back with instructions to assist the CIA agent on the scene. Because a government employee was involved in a shooting the FBI was notified and the local agent arrived as the coroner arrived to examine the scene and order the bodies removed.

The Provost Marshall Duty Officer arrived and inquired if the Beretta James was carrying was his issue weapon. James told him that he had received it from Miss Wagner when the shooting started. Megan overheard his comments and smiled thinking he had covered himself very well and stayed with his story as they were interviewed by various agencies. James surrendered the Beretta to the Provost Marshall who checked to see if it had been fired. Since it had not been, he then returned it to Megan who put it back in the range bag after insuring it was cleared and safe.

Camp Lejeune's resident NCIS agent arrived and after a minute reviewing the scene, announced he was going to let the FBI run with it but would appreciate a report once completed. He just hung around taking notes ignoring most of the people gathering around.

The FBI agent pulled an envelope out of the dead men's car which contained photos and other information on Megan. Hand written on one of the printed pages was $100K which probably was the price on Megan's head. Megan convinced the FBI agent to allow her to photograph the packet on her with her cell phone under his supervision, so the CIA would have a complete record of the contract on her. Megan never commented on the fact that nowhere in the pages or photographs was James name mentioned. She then sent the photos directly to Dotty who confirmed the receipt of each photo.

The tracking device found on the front seat lent credence to Megan's statement she felt they were being followed to the motel. Both Megan and James stated they had known each other in Japan and were reacquainting themselves when this happened. They left the rest to the imagination of those asking the questions.

The six-man CIA Security detail arrived in Marine MP Vehicles having landed at New River. Megan had been reluctant to give the FBI much information more than they had until she talked to the head of the Security detail. She knew the rules concerning a CIA officer using deadly force within the boundaries of the United States and even though she had not fired a single round in self-defense, the mattress against the window posed a lot of questions.

The local police were interviewing residents of the motel along with the desk clerk who had not witnessed the event, but did have a security camera video tape of the entire event. Megan cleaned the Tahoe of things she immediately wanted then stood back as a wrecker from Lejeune's motor pool removed the Tahoe to the base motor poll where it would later be picked up by a roll-back wrecker from the CIA's motor pool at Langley.

The Military Police had notified James' Company Commander of his involvement in a shooting and had come out to see what his command duties would require of him this night. He just stood out of the way after identifying himself to the Provost Marshall because he knew the more he was involved, the more paperwork it would create for him.

Ever since their arrival, at least one member of the Security Detail was beside Megan at all times except when she returned to her room to use the bathroom. An MP was stationed to keep track of James, but otherwise he was being ignored except to answer a few questions by the investigators. Just before the FBI released Megan and James, the head of the Security Detail received a phone call. After a minute he walked over and handed the phone to the Provost Marshall who then looked around and found James' Commander, who then talked to the individual on the other end before handing it back to the Provost Marshal. As this was happening one of the security detail moved over to James and advised the MP that James was now under the protection of the CIA.

Ten minutes later everyone was loaded up and James was taken to his barracks to pack for an undetermined stay away from the barracks. His barracks mates were interested in what was going on as James walked through the hall of his barracks followed by two men wearing all black with H&K MP-5's hanging in front of them with Federal Agent plastered across the back of their equipment vests. From the barracks, James was taken to New River where he boarded a CIA Blackhawk helicopter with Federal Government markings along with Megan and the detail for the flight back to Virginia.

They landed at the Farm's helicopter pad and were taken to one of the Guest Houses where Dotty and Dave were waiting. Megan could tell by the look on Dotty's face she was not happy. Dotty pointed to two chairs and they sat down waiting for Dotty to begin.

"First of all, I am pleased to know that neither of you were injured or had to use force to protect yourselves."

"Excuse me Ma'am, but who are you?" James inquired.

65

"Mrs. Collins is my boss James." Megan answered before Dotty could speak.

"Oh. Sorry to interrupt you Ma'am."

"No Corporal Conley, I should have insured you knew who I was before I decide if I am going to take a pound of flesh off either of you, or just be thankful you are both still alive. Megan please explain why you did not return to the safety of the base once you knew you were being followed instead of going to the motel."

"Dotty, I told you I was enroute to the motel."

"Yes, but now we have two dead critters and I am going to have to explain to my boss why they are dead during an attempt on your life."

"Sorry Dotty, I had hoped they would just sit on us through the night and maybe we could take them alive during the night."

"And the mattress against the window was part of this plan?"

"That was in case I was wrong that they would wait."

"According to the motel's night manager the two of you were making out like a couple of newlyweds at the door to the room. Hard to do much if the mattress is standing up against a wall unless you enjoy the firmness of a floor." Dotty had a slight grin on her face.

"Ma'am, Megan told me to make it look like lovers entering the room, so I took advantage of the situation and she played along with me, but once inside the room she was very professional in her actions and no further contact between us occurred."

Dave chuckled, and Dotty smiled at his comments.

"Alright, both of you relax. I'm going to tell the Director that Megan took James into protective custody because he might unknowingly have information vital to events occurring in the Far East area. If there is a contract on Megan, I'll bet a nice dinner there is one on James. The two of you will stay here until we have a determination of how to proceed. James, is your State Department security clearance still in effect?"

"I believe it is Ma'am."

"I'll confirm that later in the morning. Right now, the little brat is complaining that I'm not asleep and is making life miserable for me." She rubbed her swollen belly. "The fridge is stocked so no need to utilize the dining hall. Stay out of sight and after some sleep, each of you write an after-action report and try not to make it seem like one of you copied off the other's."

Dave helped Dotty out of her chair as Megan and Jeff stood. Dotty hugged and gave Megan a kiss on her cheek then shook James' hand. Dave just winked at Megan as he passed her to open the door for his wife. Megan watched the door close on them, looked at James then picked up her bag and headed down the hall to find a bedroom. She turned on the lights to one room then crossed the hall to find another bedroom. Megan entered that one and closed the door leaving James with the conclusion he was to take the other room. He chuckled to himself and picked up his bag and was asleep within minutes after his head hit the pillow. Megan lay in bed thinking about the kiss James had given her at the motel and how long it had been since she had shared a bed with a man. She shook off the feelings and quickly went to sleep.

Nightmares & Pancakes

Megan rolled out of bed just before eight in the morning, took a shower then only dressed in a pair of satin jogging shorts she had in her bag and pulled an oversized Special Forces embossed t-shirt on then headed for the kitchen for some coffee as she dried her hair. She hadn't even crossed the living room before she smelled sausage cooking from the kitchen. When she had left her room, she noticed the door to James' room was closed but entering the kitchen there he was, dressed in sweat pants and a tight t-shirt at the stove fixing breakfast.

She went to the coffee pot and poured herself a cup then sat down at the table watching as James dealt with fixing them something to eat. Megan never spoke to him and he just focused on the stove as she sat with her legs crossed drying her hair and watching him. He finished with the sausage patties and then poured off most of the grease from the skillet, reached for a bowel on the counter and poured eggs that had been whipped for scrambling into the skillet. A bit of salt and pepper was added as he worked the eggs to prevent them from burning. When ready he scraped them onto two plates, added two sausage patties to each plate then turned and put them on the table, one in front of her and the other further down the table away from her.

James already had toast and various jellies and jams on the table. He refilled his coffee cup and sat down, looking at her instead of eating.

"Megan, how old are you?"

"I'll be twenty-seven next month, why?"

"I'm twenty-six. I came into the Corps after my college funds ran out during my junior year. I need to ask you a personal favor while we are confined together."

"Ask away, but I'll not make you any promises."

"You are a beautiful woman and dressed as you are is distracting. Please wear pants and a bra around me. You have fantastic legs and your tits are pushing through your shirt which look extremely inviting. I find both items very distracting at this juncture in our relationship."

"Sorry, I'll go change. I didn't mean for my appearance to be a distraction."

"No, first eat while it's still hot, and then change. I'm not a prude but I have not been with a woman since Tokyo and you are certainly all woman."

Megan tasted the eggs and found them nicely done with a flavor she could not identify. Neither spoke as they ate until Megan was about half way through her plate.

"James, I'm not sure what you meant by relationship, but I never came to you thinking the night might end with us in bed. I just wanted to talk to you about the warehouse."

He never looked up as he spoke.

"Then why were you dressed like a hooker when you came to see me?"

"As I said, I'm an Army brat. I am aware of what it is like for a new man in a new assignment to not only fit in but to find companionship. You should have been decorated with a Bronze Star for that fight in the warehouse but since it was not a combat situation, no glory. So, I thought I could help set the stage for a female Marine or two to take notice of you. And from the looks some of them gave you in the mess hall, I suspect if you were in the club tonight, you'd find yourself with plenty of feminine company. If I had just picked you up wearing jeans and a blouse, no one would have noticed. Maybe I was wrong, but I've been wrong before."

Neither spoke anymore as they finished breakfast. Megan stood and took her plate to the sink then started for her room. She stopped before leaving the kitchen.

"Thank you for fixing breakfast, it was very good. I do not know who taught you to cook but they did a great job of it. I'll wash the dishes after I change."

James watched her walk away and silently cursed himself for the stiffness he had in his groin. He put his plate in the sink, refilled his cup then went to his room before Megan saw the bulge in his pants. During the last part of breakfast, he thought about the kiss they exchanged at the door and how it seemed she was not playing a scene for the benefit of the men watching them. Megan was having nearly the same thoughts as she put on a bra to cover her hard nipples remembering the kiss the night before and wondering why she had responded to it the way she did. She finished getting dressed and returned to the kitchen to wash the dishes to find James absent from the area.

It was nearly noon before Megan took the files she had been carrying and laid them out of the kitchen table. The house had a nice library and James had taken a book to his room and was reading when she knocked on his door. She noticed he had also changed his clothes and she asked him to join her in the kitchen.

As James was going through the documents she had provided, Megan laid out deli sliced ham and other items on the counter for them to make sandwiches as they worked. He asked for a notepad and made notes as he read the reports then the data on the men they had killed. Megan just sat and watched him work in silence. She only spoke to answer a question he asked otherwise it was like a monastery in the house.

Megan never thought to ask him what he had studied in college but the way he was approaching his task made her wonder just how intelligent he really was. When she was able to get a look at the notes he was making, his handwriting was neat and precise. As it got close to dinner time, she asked him if Chinese would be alright for dinner and he never looked up as he responded with a yes. She called the Farm duty officer and asked if it could be arranged. An hour later they had almost a third of the table laid out with carry out containers of Chinese food.

After she had put the left overs in the fridge, she offered him a beer which he declined. One thing she had noticed he was going through coffee like a fiend as she sipped on a glass of white wine. The only times he left his chair was to get another cup of coffee, go to the bathroom, or to move around the table to double check a document he had laid out for future reference. It was near midnight when he finally stood, stretched and looked at her sitting at the far end of the table.

"Megan, I think it is time for bed. Do I need to put this stuff up or will it be alright here tonight?"

"We can leave it here and bed sounds like a great idea."

They looked at each other and knew Freud had raised his head in that conversation and both laughed.

"I was speaking of separate beds Megan."

"I know and so was I. But you have to admit it did sound otherwise."

"Yes, but this is neither the time, nor place for such. Besides, it would do no good for either of us to entertain such thoughts."

"I agree James. Now I have to ask. What were your studying in college?"

"Chemical engineering with a minor in physics at Purdue. You?"

"History at UNC, and then International Studies at Georgetown."

"Well, goodnight Megan, I'll see you in the morning."

James left the room leaving Megan to consider what was going to happen to their lives once Langley figured out what to do with them. How would the events of the past couple day's effect his Marine career and his chances to return to college to finish his education? She went to bed dressed only in the oversize t-shirt as a nightgown.

He was awakened by sounds in the house of a woman crying. James looked at his watch to see it was nearly three-thirty in the morning and quickly slipped into his sweat pants and then took the Gerber MkII knife from his night stand that he had brought with him. Carefully he opened his door as the sounds grew louder and heard Megan scream. Her door was closed, and he moved to it then carefully opened it to see Megan thrashing on the bed in the moonlight coming through her window.

James immediately recognized what was happening as he had seen it from veteran Marines he had served with suffering from PTSD. He put the knife on the chair next to the wall and went to Megan, taking her in his arms and holding her as he softly spoke to her that everything would be alright. She fought him as he held her until she finally awoke from her nightmare. James just held her and ran his hand over her head telling her it would be alright, she was safe and not alone. Megan never spoke to him as she cried while he held her close to him until she finally went back to sleep. James leaned back against the headboard as he held her and after a time he also fell back to sleep with her in his arms.

When James woke, he was stiff from sitting up holding Megan. He looked at the clock to see it was nearly nine in the morning. James looked down at her face covered with her long hair draped over her and could only sigh at how this happened. She was completely uncovered, and her shirt had ridden up exposing her buttocks and long legs. James knew he had to get away from her, but did not want to disturb her in doing so. Just as he started to move, her left arm which was wrapped around him tighten her hold on him.

"James?"

"Yes Megan?"

"Thank you."

"Think nothing of it. Let me go before I pee all over your bed."

She released him and as he slid out from under her, she just moved on down to the pillows, pulling one in tight, never looking at him as he stood. Her bare ass was even more visible to him now, so he reached over and pulled her covers over her before turning towards the door.

"James?"

"Yes Megan?"

"Can we have pancakes for breakfast today?"

"Certainly, let me shower and get dressed. I'll knock on your door when I'm ready, so you can get up and get dressed. Pancakes are much better hot off the griddle."

"Alright James, thanks"

James picked up his knife and carefully closed the door behind him and crossed the hall. He first took a cold shower to relieve the stress in his groin then turned up the heat to clean himself. Megan lay in bed thinking about the bulge she had seen in his sweat pants trying to decide if she was feeling anything about him. No, at least not yet and his erection could be nothing more than having to empty his bladder which she knew often occurred in the morning with men.

Megan was in the shower when she heard James knock twice on her door. Her body ached from lying in such an awkward position with him during the night. James was attractive enough she thought, and his demeanor was pleasant. A chill went through her when she realized that if he had rolled her over this morning and made love to her, she would have let him.

73

Breakfast was interesting as Jeff returned to his study of the documents as they ate. He never made a single comment about her nightmares when they did talk. Megan did the dishes as he was making notes going from one page to another then back again. She wondered if he was seeing something that they had missed.

"James, what's wrong?"

"Megan, it still does not make sense that they were going to hijack that shipment of seed. What would they have done with it once out of the warehouse? Who would have benefitted from the thief?"

"One theory was they were going to sell it to the North Koreans since they are having a worse time than the South feeding their people."

"Look, I know the Japanese Police have told us those folks were Communists but the profiles you have here on those men clearly show they are capitalists. Sure, a capitalist can make money off a communist but there is also a price for doing business with those folks and that's the risk of being put out of business later on by your customer. Maybe I'm over simplifying the whole thing, but I am having problem with that theory."

"Okay Jeff, keep looking, you never know what you might find."

"Megan, I've gone through these reports until I'm seeing cross eyed. No, I'm done here. But whatever we do discover will not be what we think. I'm certain of that."

Neither spoke as he carefully collected up the documents, making sure they were in order as he put them back in their file folders. Once finished he left them for her to deal with as he took a cup of coffee out onto the screened in back porch. Megan stood at the door looking out at him sitting on a patio chair just staring off into the woods behind them. She decided to see if there was anything on television worth watching and went into the living room. She got in on the very first of an old Doris Day movie and watched it. Megan looked at the clock above the television and thought about lunch. When she stood and turned, Jeff was standing behind her chair which startled her.

"Megan, I've given this a lot of thought so please let me speak my mind before you say anything. We have not known each other very long and the conditions of our relationship have been stressful. There is a lot of sexual tension between us whether we want to admit it or not, and that kiss in front of the motel room only makes it worse."

He paused as if collecting his thoughts.

"The first time I saw you I had this vision of you laid across my bed, exhausted from being made love too, but let's be honest here, you are a very desirable woman and I'm a normal red-blooded man. Any thoughts we, especially I have had concerning a relationship more than what is proper is most likely based on the fact that we have survived two very dangerous situations and not the normal sexual attraction of two individuals who have met at a party. Once we have gotten past the understanding of why we are feeling what we do, we can move on and get this job done in finding those folks that want to see us in a coffin."

"James, you said that you have not been with a woman since Japan. It has been even longer for me with a man. Yes, I believe you are right in your assessment of this situation. Now that it is out in the open, I believe we can move on without the tension between us. And I want to thank you for not taking advantage of me during the night or this morning. I was incapable of stopping you if you had."

He looked at her for a moment then turned and went into the kitchen. She followed him, and they talked about the problem of why they were marked for death as they made sandwiches for lunch. Megan could still tell something was bothering him, but left it alone as they worked through his notes. But what was bothering him would come to light later in the day.

They received a message from Dotty that they would be brought to Langley in the morning and to be ready by 0600 hours. Megan had only packed a small bag and needed to wash her clothes. She told James what she had to do, and he told her to get busy which caused her to laugh. Megan stripped down to her jogging shorts and oversize t-shirt as she used the washer and dryer in the house. James had stayed in his room reading as she was dealing with this detail but as she was carrying her clean laundry to her room he met her in the hall. He just stood looking her in her eyes.

"James, what's wrong?"

"Tomorrow, are you going to tell Dotty about your nightmares, or shall I?"

"James…"

"Don't James me Megan. I know what you are going through and I refuse to stand by and watch as you come apart at the seams. The stress of the warehouse fight, the ambush and now the attempt on your life again is wearing on you. I need a partner I can depend on and you have already admitted that you could not defend yourself this morning."

"Since when are we partners?"

"Since you placed that Beretta in my hands two nights ago. We are partners until told otherwise even if I no longer have that Beretta in hand."

Megan just stared at him and he never flinched nor turned away from her glare. She stepped past him and went into her room dumping her laundry on her bed. She picked up the Beretta range bag from the foot of her bed and just threw it at him. He caught it and continued to look at her. Megan was fuming at what he had said but inside it was eating away at her personal defenses until she sat down on the edge of the bed and began to cry. She knew he was right in that she was scared, and it was bringing out the nightmares of what she had done and survived. All her life this had been a game for her to achieve in, excel in, but now it was real, and she was becoming unsure she could deal with the consequences of her own actions.

James walked to her, sat the bag down then kneeled in front of her. He lifted her head up to look at her and for her to look at him.

"Megan, I watched my father suffer as you are now from his experiences in Vietnam. It drove him nearly insane until he took his own life when I was nine years old. I've also had the nightmares, but I know why I am having them and know how to deal with them. Maybe not the best answer but I have been able to deal with them without alcohol or drugs. Being scared is normal, but do not allow it to control you."

She looked at him as the tears rolled down her cheeks as she gained control of her crying and breathing.

"Alright, I'll talk to Dotty in the morning."

"Good, now get your act together and put your clothes up before they get all wrinkled. You up for Italian tonight?"

Megan smiled. "Yes, Italian sounds great."

James pulled her head down and kissed her on the forehead before he stood, retrieved the bag and left her alone. She put her clothes up and laid down on her bed considering what he had said to her. Had her father felt the things she was feeling and if so, how had he dealt with them, so she never saw the results? As she slowly fell asleep she came to recognize the only thing wrong with her was that she was more normal than she had ever admitted to herself. She felt a wave of relief over her as she knew she could control and live with her fears as long as she had a goal in mind which was more important than herself.

After Megan had awakened for supper, she just stayed to herself as she considered her life and the effects of her nightmares. James read in the living room as she stayed busy for a time cleaning the house. He knew there wasn't much to deal with but left her alone as he had seen his mother do the same thing when she had serious things on her mind.

The trip to Langley was also quiet as they sat beside each other in the armored Denali with security vehicles in front and back of them. Both were armed and ready if the need occurred. Getting James through the security at Langley was easier than Megan had anticipated with Dotty arranging for his access pass and Dave meeting them to speed things up.

Dotty introduced James to the crew and once that was completed turned James over to Tyler to set up the part where James was going to brief everyone on what he made notes on. Megan followed Dotty back to her desk and ask for a few minutes with her to talk about a personal problem. When Dotty motioned for her to take the seat next to her desk, the rest of the Dungeon crew moved away, knowing this had to be a private conversation, and gave them all the room the possible.

Megan looked back at James before she sat down, and he winked at her which seemed to give her the strength for the task ahead. Dotty sat quietly and listened as Megan told her about the nightmares and even admitted a sense of failure because of what she was feeling. When she finished, Megan actually felt a sense of relief in that it was now out in the open, at least open to Dotty, her boss. Dotty waited a moment or two before she called Dave over and asked him to open his shirt to allow Megan to see the scars from a shotgun blast that nearly killed him.

"Megan, those scars were caused by a terrorist that tried to kill Dave and myself with a shotgun one afternoon." Dotty moved her chair over so Megan could see Dotty's right leg as she raised her skirt up to expose the scars she also carried. "These scars come from the same shotgun as I was moving away from Dave, separating ourselves to make it harder on the shooter. I put two bullets into the shooter's chest, but he was wearing body armor and he got the shot off before my third shot hit him in the face. We both know what it is like to be scared and under fire. You are not alone here."

"I knew Bill had been a Ranger and wounded in combat, but not this about the two of you. James has spoken to me about my problem and I think, no, I believe I can deal with it now that I'm no longer trying to hide it from those around me."

"Megan, you are very well trained to do a job that is full of violence. If you cannot come to grips with the possibilities of your job, then find a new one. Granted, there are field officers who go their entire career without ever being exposed to the dangers you have but you have found yourself in a situation that has never been considered in training. We're here anytime you want to talk. Alright?"

"Yes Dotty, I understand."

"Good, it looks like James is about ready to start his brief."

Gretchen had made copies of James' notes for everyone and they followed him through his brief of what he considered important. When he hit upon something they had already considered but eliminated by information he did not have at hand, it was pointed out to him and he discussed the answer the crew had determined, and only once did he challenge the answer which sent the crew back to reexamine that answer after his brief was over.

James received several comments concerning the quality of his brief and his view of the information he had reviewed. There were still questions to be answered and Ron took him in hand as they looked at the white board, trying to connect a few dots James might help with. Megan also noticed that Kathy was hovering near James as he moved from board to board examining what work was already done.

One thing James noticed about the people he was dealing with was they never asked what he did in the Marines or his rank. They accepted him as he presented himself and listened without prejudice to his conclusions. Any debate concerning a point different from their own was done in a manner of respect and inquiry, not one of self-importance.

After lunch, Gretchen was taken to Megan's condo along with William and Clifton to pack several bags for Megan, so she would have other clothing available to her at the Farm. Dotty determined that for their own security, Megan and James were to remain at the Farm and the computer system at the house was to be linked to the Dungeon along with the ability to video chat.

When Megan asked why James was remaining with her at the Farm, Dotty stated that the FBI had discovered through a confidential informant that he also had a contract on his head. Having them work from the Farm reduced their exposure. By the time they returned to the Farm, CIA IT technicians had upgraded the guest house to include white boards and cork boards.

Down on the Farm

James received orders from Headquarters Marine Corps seconding him to the CIA for the duration of the operation at the discretion of the Director of the CIA. Megan could tell that James was not pleased with the prospect of being confined with her, but took his assignment like a Marine and carried on with it. Megan joked a few days after they had returned to the farm that Kathy seemed to be interested in him. His reply took her by surprise when he said she was attractive, but he preferred a brunette over redhead.

Before the end of the week both of them were developing cabin fever with just work and sleep. Megan suggested they not only get some outside exercise but hit the ranges from time to time. The next morning they ran for two miles with Megan setting the pace after doing some stretching exercises and sit ups. On the pistol ranges Megan notice James was steady with the Beretta but his scores were not what she expected. She was polite in asking him if he had a problem with handguns and his reply was even though he had large hands, he did not feel comfortable with the Beretta even though he had qualified as an expert with one.

Megan had him try her Sig P250C and he did a little better but still not as good as he even felt he could do. He said the grip felt a bit small in his hand. Since James now had a CIA license to carry a firearm, Megan took him to the Farm's armory and had him handle several different handguns until he said the Sig P226 felt the best of all of them. The armorer set him up with a P226 in 40 S&W plus holsters along with two hundred and fifty rounds of ammunition for range firing and one hundred rounds of hollow points for his carry. The next day his scores improved, and he seemed more comfortable with the Sig, even if his scores never reached Megan's.

William and Clifton brought Megan's rebuilt Tahoe to her with a few additions. Bullet resistant glass had been installed along with Kevlar liners in all the doors. They also brought all of James' uniforms and personal items from Camp Lejeune.

In the back of the Tahoe, under the carpet was a hide-away containing a pair of H&K MP-5's with five magazines each and an over the shoulder bag for the extra magazines. William told them they were to hang onto them until they were released from their protective custody. Two ammunition cans were also in the back containing one thousand rounds of 147 grain Full Metal Jacket for them to train with plus use as the primary round for the weapons. The next day they hit the ranges and burned up almost one hundred rounds each with James slightly edging her out on score.

Megan noticed an improvement in James behavior after spending time on the ranges, but something was still bothering him. At the house he spent hours going through the photos of the warehouse that had recently been updated but as he eliminated one photo after another from the list, he still studied over twenty daily as if he had missed something the first dozen times he had examined them.

One morning after a four-mile run, Megan took a shower as was normal for both of them. But instead of going directly in his room and showering, James went to the boards to look at something he had thought about during the run. He made a note to the white board and decided it was time to shower. As he walked down the hall he noticed Megan's door was not fully closed and through the slight opening, he could see Megan standing just outside the bathroom drying her hair. She was nude and standing at an angle away from him but all that could be seen was all any man would wish to see. He took a step to the door, grabbed the door knob and jerked it hard shut. Megan was startled by the sound of her door slamming shut and realized it must not have been closed because James never opened her door without knocking first and waiting for a response.

After she dressed, Megan went to the kitchen to make French toast for breakfast as they had decided on during their run. James finally came into the kitchen, poured a cup of coffee and went directly to the computer and pulled up the photos he considered important. He never spoke to her and she decided to let him bring up the open door. When she had his ready, she took it to him and sat it down out of his way as he was writing. He looked over at the plate then up at her and told her thanks, then went back to writing. Megan sat at the kitchen table where she could watch him work as she ate. When he finished with breakfast he continued writing just moving the plate out of the way. Megan collected his plate and once again he thanked her.

It was nearly noon when he picked up another pad and referencing his notes on the first once more began to write. Megan was becoming concerned that he was becoming obsessed with finding out why they were marked for death. He had only been out of that chair long enough to refill his coffee cup or to use the toilet. James finally stood, stretched and then went into the kitchen to refill his cup. From there he went out the kitchen door to the screened in back patio and just stood looking out its door towards the woods behind the house.

Megan went to the desk and read his notes.

Question: Why are there contracts on Megan and myself? Answer: Because we must have seen something without realizing it which places whomever is involved at risk. Revenge could apply while in Japan or Korea but very expensive here in the states.

Question: Why were there no warehouse employees present during the attack on us? Answer: Because they were all at a safety meeting at the time of the incident. Could the manager who called that meeting been involved in whatever was going to happen in the warehouse that we interrupted, or did we interrupt anything but came in after the fact?

Question: Where was the warehouse security officer? Answer: He was assisting other security officers in removing a gang of juveniles from the docks on the back side of the warehouse. Bad timing or planned?

Question: Megan's appearance is Japanese, but she is taller than most Japanese women and was with an American, but the only man to speak to her spoke in Japanese even though the profile

83

on that man says he spoke good English. Answer: He spoke Japanese because he assumed she was native even though she had an American with her. Did he know in advance who he was speaking to?

Question: Was Megan's Korean assignment involved in the attack? Answer: Unknown, although two of her Field Agents had disappeared the month prior to the attack. Could they be related?

Question: How did two small time hoods from Baltimore get their hands on an expensive and highly technical tracking device to place on Megan's vehicle and use it to track her location? Answer: Unknown.

Question: How long with Megan and myself be secluded from the rest of the planet and how will it affect my career as a Marine? Answer: Unknown.

Megan pulled her cell phone from her back pocket and took a photo of the list before he tore it up as he often did. She walked to the door to the patio and just stood watching him as he sipped his coffee staring out into nothing. Megan felt sorry for him in that if she was the original target in Japan, then he was a victim of collateral damage. She went out onto the patio but stayed slightly behind him so as not to interrupt his thoughts. Almost immediately he spoke to her.

"I'm alright Megan. I just wish things were different."

"What things James?"

"All I wanted to do was be a Marine. Save my money and go back to school and get my degrees, find a decent job and hopefully a good woman to love and grow old with. I turned down Officer's Candidate School because I never figured on making the Corps a career but if I had, I wouldn't be here now. I wish I knew why someone out there wants us dead. I could deal with not knowing who wants us gone, but what really bothers me is we're missing something simple and I dislike not knowing."

"James, I don't like this either and I am so sorry I drug you into this. I really am."

"Meg, you came to me looking for answers that we both probably have, but do not know where to find them. If you had not come to me, there are good odds I'd be dead by now once whoever is behind this figured out where I was stationed. In a way you saved my life both at the motel and most likely later. Don't be sorry, because I'm not."

"What do we do now?"

"Hun, we keep looking and asking questions until there are no more questions to ask. With the Dungeon having to put this task aside to work on higher priority projects, we are all we have to find the answers needed to keep us alive."

He turned to face her.

"Megan, the first time we met I was tasked to protect you and we protected each other. I will not stop looking for the answers because if I cannot protect you in one way, I'll do so anyway I can."

Before she could speak he turned back to the view of the woods. What he had said struck a chord with her. He all but said he was willing to die to protect her but was it from a sense of duty or something else. She could not think of a thing to say or do which could relieve the pressure he had to be feeling and seeing her through the open door most likely did not help his situation.

Megan left him to his thoughts and went back into the kitchen considering what to fix for lunch. She was in turmoil on what to do about their situation until she remembered the memory stick. What would be gained by opening the last folder? What price came with opening that file? She looked back out at James and decided no price was too high if he was willing to put such a priority on her own life. Megan went to her room and removed the stick from her purse and fingered it for a minute before heading back to the living room and inserting the stick into the computer.

Once everything was loaded she just sat and looked at the final icon flashing on the monitor. Her finger paused on the mouse as she once more considered the unknown price she might have to pay for pushing down on the mouse. But it also dawned on her that Gunner Grainger had presented the stick to her. From everything she had heard about him, she doubted he would purposely put her directly in the line of fire. She did the left click on the icon and waited.

Seconds after she clicked on the icon the printer began to print out a page. Nothing happened on the monitor until the page finished printing then the monitor went black, then back to the desktop. Megan wondered what happened until she removed the page from the printer and read what was printed on it.

NOTICE: This file cannot be opened on an uncoded computer. Text shipping information via 1-888-555-0000. Any further attempt to open this file with an uncoded computer will cause the file to wipe itself clean.

Megan removed the memory stick and shoved it into her jeans pocket. Her interest in the final file was building and once more she trusted that Grainger would not lead her astray. She pulled her cell phone from her back pocket and typed in her name, the address of the guest house and the number given on the paper. She never paused as she hit send. All she could do now was wait to see the results of her desperation.

She went back to the kitchen and looked in the fridge trying to decide what to fix for lunch. James came in as she stood there and put his hand on hers as it rested on the fridge door.

"What do say about heading over to the dining hall and let someone else do the cooking and dish washing?"

"How about some range time afterwards? Maybe the H&K's?"

"Megan, that sounds like a great way to burn off a ton of frustration. Grab your range bag and let's go. I'm buying lunch."

She laughed knowing neither of them had to pay to eat in the Farm's dining hall.

That night Megan made sure her door was closed as she readied herself for bed. She went to sleep hoping that she had made the right decision by sending the text. Megan had not had a nightmare since the one which James came to her aid but tonight one came to her in a manner she would have never considered awake. She was wounded and crawling towards the only man she considered the love of her life as his own body was leaking its life blood from his wounds. She awoke screaming his name. She awoke to see James standing in her door, back lite by the hallway lights looking at her,

"I'm alright James, honest I am. It was a nightmare from my youth."

"Really? Was there a James in your youth?"

"Why would you ask that?"

"Because you were calling my name in your nightmare, so I came to see if you were in distress."

"Sorry, I do not remember you in my dreams or nightmares." She lied.

"Goodnight then Megan, and please, if I am to continue coming to your room at night, please wear panties to bed." He stepped back and closed the door.

Megan looked down at herself and realized she was exposed in the faint light. She laughed then lay back down and went back to sleep.

Spilled Rice

James was gone when Megan got up. The door to his room was open and he was not to be found in the house. She checked the doors and found the back door leading off the patio unlocked. Megan took a cup of coffee and sat on the back patio, waiting for his return. At least she hoped he returned.

It was after nine before she saw him step out of the woods dressed in his Marine digitals with his Sig in his drop leg holster and his MP-5 hanging in front of him by its single point sling. His pace was easy as he came to the house and entered the patio. Megan stood and looked at him; his face seemed weary as he looked at her.

"Are you hungry James?"

"Starving."

"Get cleaned up while I fix you some breakfast."

He never said another word as he passed her heading for his room.

They never spoke as they ate a late breakfast nor afterwards as he did the dishes. When he had finished he went to his room, collected the book he had been reading and just sat in the big easy chair in the living room, reading. Megan decided to do a load of laundry when there was a knock on the front door. She had her Sig in her hand as James opened the door to find one of the security officers standing there with a large FedEx overnight package in hand for Megan. James accepted it and placed it on the coffee table after thanking the guard for the delivery.

Megan put her laundry on the kitchen table and went to see what was in the package. The return label said it came from a gift shop in Scottsdale, Arizona. She pulled the switchblade from her right rear pocket and opened the package. It contained a new laptop, a cell phone and what the label said was a Wi-Fi connection device. There was a sealed envelope which once opened had instructions on how to use the Wi-Fi connection. She took everything to her room and set up on the desk in it and turned the computer on. It powered up normal and Megan retrieved the memory stick once again from her purse and inserted it into a USB port.

What came up on the screen sent a chill up her spine. A list of instructions for the use of the package in order to obtain intelligence required to perform services in defense of the United States. Megan followed the instructions to insure the Wi-Fi had a good connection and then opened the webpage indicated on the instruction page. She was given an email address along with a password she could remember. This would be her personal email to conduct business with any of the list of people shown in her email contact list. The names in the contact list were almost comical in construction but this was what she was given to work with.

Megan picked a name then started to compose an email but was lost at what to say. She thought for time then decided to place James' list in the email and see what response she might receive. When she hit send, it only took a second to get a confirmation of it being sent. She closed the webpage and began to read the remainder of the file. Once she shut down the computer the memory stick would wipe itself clean and the only way to get to the classified portion of the computer was via one of the loaded games using the password for the email site. From that point on, everything would be automatic each time she entered the coded portion of the computer.

The cell phone was an inexpensive LG Flip-phone which when she turned it on she received a text message stating email received, you will be contacted. When she looked in the phones memory, the phone number of the phone made even less sense than the email address. It was only five numbers long and nowhere could she find any other information. She left it turned on and slipped it into her front pocket. After she turned off the computer, she took the memory stick into the living room and inserted it into that computer and smiled when the stick showed to be completely clean of data.

Megan made sure she had the information on the information page memorized before she tore it into little pieces and flushed them down the toilet. As she was watching the water circle in the toilet bowel she realized she had turned twenty-seven without fanfare the day before. She thought back to the events of the previous year and wondered if she would see her next birthday. Megan missed talking to her parents on those days but remembered she was told not to contact them and she was told that they had been advised of her situation and not to try to make contact with her. This confused her, but she had accepted that she was no longer in control of her own life at this point.

The next week was day after day of the same to the point they were becoming bored. They ran in the mornings and the ranges in the afternoon for an hour. James never went back to the computer except to check if any new information had been sent to them overnight and she checked it in the evenings. He spent his time in the easy chair reading and she finally started reading War and Peace to try to make the days go by faster. Twice during this time James had been gone when she awoke to return later in the morning after a long walk in the woods surrounding the house. Megan never spoke to him about his walks but waited for him on the patio to return.

Six days after she had received the laptop, they were reading after cleaning up after lunch when there was a knock on the door. Megan opened the door to see an older black man whom she thought she recognized standing there smiling.

"Can I help you?" She asked.

"No, but I might be able to help you. May I come in?"

She stood back from the door and as she turned to James he wasn't in his chair then she noticed he was off to the side with his pistol in hand watching the door. Megan suddenly realized she had forgotten their protective situation, but he hadn't and was prepared for a fight. The gentleman stepped through the door and without looking at James spoke to him.

"Corporal Conley, you have no need for that. Holster it before you hurt someone."

"Who are you before I even consider putting this away?"

The black man reached into his shirt pocket and removed an ID card which he handed to Megan. She looked at it then nodded to James who put the Sig away and reached for the offered card from Megan.

"Alright Master Sergeant Lucas, what's your business here with Megan?" Jeff asked.

"Actually, I am here for both of you." He turned to Megan. "You certainly look better than the last time we met. I think I like the shorter hair on you better, but times are different now."

Megan suddenly realized who he was. He was her evaluator from the Fort Leonard Wood exercise.

"Yes, I remember you now. Can I offer you a cup of coffee while you explain how you can help us?"

They went to the kitchen and sat at the table with James taking a position as widely separated from Megan as possible. Lucas smiled as he looked back and forth at them before speaking.

"First of all, something for you from your parents." He spoke to Megan as he opened his jacket and removed a colored envelope and handed it to her.

She immediately knew what it was and opened it to find a nice birthday card in it with a note written on the inside wishing her a happy birthday and for her to take care of herself. She put the card back into the envelope as she fought the tears trying to develop in her eyes.

"Thank you, Master Sergeant."

"You're welcome and both of you please call me Mark. I'm retired now. Next, we have some information for Corporal Conley. Marine, tomorrow you will be visited by a couple of Marines from Headquarters, Marine Corps who will interview you and give you a long, written test to take. I suggest you get a good night's sleep and be ready for it. It's important to you and the Corps."

"What kind of test and must you keep referring to me as Corporal?"

"No, I was just having a bit of fun James. Damn, you need to relax before you have a stroke. If I was going to harm either one of you, you'd both already be dead."

Lucas reached into his trousers pocket and removed two large gold coins and handed one over to Megan and slid the other to James. They both looked at them turning them over to examine both sides. James was puzzled by coin since it was for a Marine Recon Chief Gunnery Warrant Officer Five, but Megan suddenly laughed.

"James, he's right. Relax. We have friends in dark places."

James looked at Megan and laid the coin down and picked up his coffee cup. It was apparent to him that she was in charge and he just sat waiting for the other shoe to drop.

Lucas reached into the lower pocket of his jacket and removed a small, padded envelope and handed it to her.

"In there you will find the answers to the questions you asked. They created a bit of a problem at first which is why it took as long as it did for me to deliver them. Try to keep your questions simpler the next time."

Lucas took another drink of coffee then stood.

"Keep those coins on you at all times. They are better than a CIA ID card in some places. Good day, and I will see you again in time."

Lucas never gave them a chance to respond as he quickly moved out of the kitchen then out of the house. James followed him and looked out the door as Lucas got into the front seat of a Marine Corps staff car that had a covered license plate on the front. He knew only those of flag rank had license plates mounted in such a fashion. He had some General's car, but which General? He turned back to look at Megan, but she was not in sight, so he went to her room to find her at the small desk opening the laptop.

"What's going on Megan?"

"James, I may have just made a deal with the devil." She spoke without looking at him.

Megan had two high density memory sticks on the desk marked '1' and '2'. Once the computer was booted up she plugged the first stick into the USB and it automatically opened. There was a very large folder marked as 'Warehouse Photos' on it with a WordPad note which when she opened that page, it told how to transfer the encrypted files to standard files, so they could view them on the larger monitor. They found a blank CD and transferred the files in compressed form to it and then went to the computer in the living room to load them for viewing.

Immediately James recognized there were more photos than they already had by over a third. Megan could tell this caught his attention as he took over and edited them, moving the ones he had already eliminated into a holding folder as not to lose them as he viewed any new ones. Megan went back to the laptop and opened the other stick and read the files. She decided to wait until James had viewed the photos before talking to him about the files contents.

James worked through dinner eating pizza at the computer Megan had ordered from the Farm's Dining Hall. Megan just sat on the couch reading, staying out of his way but there in case he needed something. She would notice from time to time he would go back to a set of photos that to her, seemed to have nothing to do with the assault on them but they interested him.

It was after eight in the evening when he chuckled out loud and turned his chair towards her.

"Grab a chair and come see what I've found."

Megan pulled up another office chair beside his as he moved over so she could clearly see what he was looking at. On the screen was a photo looking down the row of stacked grain seeds with no individuals present in the photo. It took her a moment to notice the pile of grain on the floor next to the stack of grain.

"James, are you thinking that spillage is important?"

"Yes, it is. Watch."

He put up another photo that was taken of the pile of grain and in the photo, it showed five layers of sacks.

"Now Megan, think about this for a minute. If there was spillage shouldn't there be an open grain sack or at least one that has been resewn but deflated if you will due to the loss of the seed?"

"Yes, I guess so."

"Good, now look at the third sack up from the floor. The stitching is wrong. It has been repaired but it is nearly as full as the other sacks around it."

"Yes Jeff, that makes sense. So, what are you thinking?"

"First of all, I don't think we interrupted a hijacking. I think we interrupted a smuggling operation. Open a sack, remove some grain, stuff whatever you want to smuggle into Korea into it then put what grain you need back into the sack and sew it back up."

James put another photo up on the screen that showed a stack of grain. He took a pencil and started pointing out specific sacks within the stack. All appeared to have been repaired yet full of grain.

"Another thing Megan, those Field Agents that came up missing before you went to Japan. What was their function over there? What did they do besides spying for you?"

"They were both involved in distribution. Oh damn, James, maybe they discovered the smuggling and were killed because of it!"

"My thinking also Doll. Plus, I would bet a pay check that not only did we interrupt the operation, we walked into a trap designed to kill you in case you knew or suspected the smuggling operation. Otherwise, why kill the driver before attacking us?"

"My God James, that's brilliant! I mean the way you are putting this together makes much more sense than anything we have come up with yet."

Megan leaned over and wrapped her arms around his neck and hugged him tight. He put his arms around her and returned the hug but when she started to pull away from him, she stopped and kissed him. James responded to the kiss as she pulled him tighter to her lips. When they finally broke the kiss she leaned back, releasing him as he just let her nearly slide from his arms until his hands were at her waist. They looked at each other, neither willing to speak. Afraid of saying what they both knew had to be said.

James stood, leaned over and picked her up out of the chair as if she was a child ready to be carried to bed. Megan wrapped her arms around his neck again and kissed him. This time there was no hiding the passion between them. When she broke the kiss, James carried her to her bedroom, laid her on her bed, and then joined her.

Megan woke to find herself alone in bed. She looked at the clock on the nightstand and saw it was 0613 in the morning. Her body ached from the use of it last night and she snuggled back into the pillows, smelling James' sweat on the one he had slept on. Even before he picked her up from the chair she knew in her heart she was in love with him. Megan felt he had the same feelings for her but neither of them spoke such words during the night as they made love twice before exhaustion took them into sleep.

Her bladder began to complain as she rose from the bed, she noticed her door was closed and it had been open when they fell asleep. Megan smiled as she looked at herself in the mirror thinking how the marks on her breasts came about. She put on her oversized t-shirt, brushed out her hair and went looking for James. As soon as she opened her door, she found him standing in his bedroom, fixing the tie to his dress green uniform. She walked over and leaned against his door frame watching him get himself squared away.

"Baby, about last night."

"James, don't say it. We both have wanted it to happen for some time now. I have no complaints or regrets."

"Megan, all I was going to say was I really enjoyed last night. You are a fantasy come true for a man like me."

"A man like you? James, you grossly under estimate yourself. But let's not travel down that conversational path. Last night we expended a lot of frustration and lust but tonight will tell us both just how things will be between us as long as we are together."

He stopped what he was doing and looked at her. She could see the indecision in his eyes and she smiled at him.

"James, let's just take this day to day. Enjoy each other and let's see what happens when this is all over with. Alright?"

"Alright Megan, now get dressed before company arrives. No telling what time they will get here, and we still need to eat after expending all that energy last night."

Megan laughed, turned to go back to her room and pulled up the back of her shirt to flash him. She heard him laughing as she closed the door to her room and laid out her clothes. As she dressed she changed her mind on the blouse she was going to wear and instead put on form fitting tank top and covered it with one of her Father's old plaid shirts. This concealed her Sig which she did not want anyone to see today. Megan thought about James in his uniform and retrieved her Sig P238 from her purse, double checked to insure it was ready to go and went into the kitchen where he as sitting, drinking coffee.

"Here, put this in a pocket where you can get to it if needed."

"Megan, I don't know."

"Neither do I Darling, but as the saying goes, better safe than full of bullet holes."

James laughed, checked the pistol before putting it into his right pants pocket after transferring the gold coin to his left. Megan gave him a quick kiss then went to make French toast for breakfast. After breakfast, they wrote the report for the Dungeon based on what James had discovered and the possibilities of that discovery. Once that was sent, she went to her laptop and wrote a request for information concerning the frequency of juvenile gangs running on the docks requiring security guards to be away from their posts. Dates and times of shipments from those warehouses to Korea. Additional information concerning safety briefings for warehouse personal. Fifteen minutes after she sent the request, her flip phone vibrated in her pocket. The message said '36 hours' minimum to recover'.

At 0845 a Marine staff car pulled up in front of the guest house. James put his uniform blouse on and squared himself away as Megan shut down the computer in the living room and removed all documents from sight. The cork and white boards were covered with sheets and all they could do now was wait for the knock on the door. Megan watched as a Full Colonel along with what she determined to be a Master Gunnery Sergeant got out of the car and carrying briefcases came up the walk. The driver just stood looking around before sitting back down in the front seat and waited.

James greeted the two Marines at the door and invited them in. Colonel Walker introduced himself and then introduced Master Gunnery Sergeant Crenshaw. It was quickly determined the kitchen would be the best place to take care of business with its large table so they could deal with some paperwork after a short interview. Megan played the hostess getting them situated and coffee as they talked.

Being an Army brat, she thought it was a bit ungentlemanly of the Colonel leaving his driver out in the cool weather and decided to bring him into the house. Just as she reached the door she could see the driver out of the car and taking photos with his cell phone. She positioned herself at the door, looking through the window and watched him also take photos of her Tahoe to include the license plate. When he finished that, the driver reached into the car and it appeared he reached under the front seat for something then moved to her Tahoe and placed a small, black object under the front bumper of her truck. Once that was done, he sat back down in the driver's seat and it looked as if he was texting someone.

Megan moved back into the kitchen where she had a clear field of fire on the two Marines from their rear, looked at James with a grin on her face as she drew her Sig. James dropped his hands to his lap not knowing what was going on but following her lead.

"Gentlemen, be very quiet and carefully place both of your hands on top of the table. I won't ask twice."

The Marines looked back at her to see the Sig pointed in their direction then they heard James's chair scrape the floor as he stood with the small Sig in his large hands. Both immediately put their hands on the table with the Colonel becoming irritated.

"What's the meaning of this Corporal Conley?"

"I think you need to be asking Miss Wagner that question Colonel. She's in command here, Sir."

"Colonel Walker, I just witnessed your driver taking photos of this house and my vehicle to include its license plate. He then placed an object under the front bumper of my Tahoe then started sending text messages from the actions I could observe. Now do you care to tell me what is going on or do I go outside and possibly kill him if he resists?"

"Excuse me a moment please" The Master Gunny spoke as he slowly stood. "I'm going to reach into my trousers pocket for something that may help some here." He slowly reached into his pocket and when his came out he tossed a large gold coin on the table in front of James. James looked at it, reached into his left pocket and tossed his coin on the table.

"Megan, it seems we have a friend in court today." James spoke.

"So it does, but it still does not answer my question about why the driver is taking photos and placing devices on my truck."

"Miss Wagner, how about me going out there and collecting him up for you. Tell him to come in and have some coffee since we are going to be here awhile." Suggested Crenshaw.

"Yes, please, I really wish to talk to him." Megan responded.

Crenshaw looked at the Colonel. "Colonel, unless you have one of those coins in your pocket, may I suggest you keep quiet. Miss Wagner has already killed three men in the past year and Colonel, I really doubt she'll worry too much about killing you."

He picked up his cover from the table and walked by Megan as if she wasn't there. Megan moved behind him to the side of the door after he had gone through it and waited. James sat back down with his hands on the table covering the pistol with his free hand. A couple minutes later the driver entered the door with Crenshaw behind him. Before Megan could do anything, Crenshaw had the Sergeant in a very uncomfortable position and unable to defend himself in any manner.

"Miss Wagner, do you have anything to tie him up with?"

"I'll be right back." Megan ran to her room and retrieved several zip ties from her range bag and together they tied the driver's hands behind his back and his feet together as he protested his treatment. As he lay on the floor, Crenshaw emptied his pockets and checked him carefully to insure he had nothing in which to harm them. Once completed, they placed him on the couch as he was becoming more vocal concerning a senior NCO laying hands on a junior NCO. Crenshaw went into the kitchen, picked up a dishtowel and returned to stuff it in his mouth to shut him up.

Back in the kitchen, Crenshaw picked up his coin returning it to his pocket before speaking.

"Miss Wagner, Corporal Conley, my purpose here today was to insure the process that the Colonel was to execute was done properly and by the book. As the Colonel can confirm, I have no working relationship with him at Headquarters, Marine Corps. I'm actually stationed at Quantico as the acting Sergeant Major of the Warrant Officer School. I stand ready to assist you in discussing the nature of this business with the Colonel, but I must stand aside unless specifically needed in all other matters."

Megan had the Colonel stand and empty his pockets onto the table before she frisked him from ankles to his collar. She was not gentle when checking his crotch for any hidden items stashed there. Once she had him seated she told him to keep his hands on top of the table unless otherwise told to move them. Megan stood to the side out of reach and started the questioning.

"Colonel Walker, how well do you know your driver?"

"Miss Wagner, I don't know him. I was told my usual driver had the flu and Sergeant Books would be driving me today. What is going on here?"

Megan looked at Crenshaw. "How can we confirm this?"

Crenshaw pulled his cell phone from inside his uniform blouse and smiled. "It'll only take a minute or three." He stepped to the patio door and made a call. No one spoke as he quietly talked then hung up.

"This may take a bit longer, it seems his driver is married and lives out on the economy."

Megan nodded then picked up the driver's phone she had brought in and began to do a search of its photo album. She then checked messages sent and saw that every photo had been sent to the same phone number. She pulled her flip phone out and sent a message asking for owner of the number on the driver's phone. She said it was urgent, priority one. She received a reply almost immediately telling her to 'stand by'. Three minutes later she had a reply and she did not like it at all. 'Owner unknown, phone purchased with cash at a Dollar General Store two days ago.'

She thought about the possibilities for a couple minutes then used her regular phone to call the Farm Security Office requesting a detail to take an individual into custody and bomb disposal to check her Tahoe. The response was immediate. The Security detail took the driver into custody as the bomb disposal team inspected her truck. The device the driver had planted was a tracking device, not an explosive device. It was activated and transmitting.

Megan was going to play a hunch. Whoever was on the receiving end of the photo texts would not be fooled if they moved the transmitter to another location. She asked the security detail to arrange moving them to different quarters while leaving her Tahoe on location. Security went right to work moving the business end of Megan's operation while they finished up with the Marine Colonel.

Crenshaw had received the information he had requested as Megan was talking to the Security detail and when she reentered the kitchen, the atmosphere seemed calmer with the Colonel talking to Jeff about his future in the Marines. They talked for almost twenty minutes before the Colonel's cell phone buzzed. After he hung up he looked at Crenshaw then Jeff.

"Corporal Conley, that was the Commandant. He apologized for not getting back to me sooner after Master Gunnery Sergeant Crenshaw's call, but he was in a meeting with the Joint Chiefs."

The Colonel picked up his brief case placing it on the table and opened it. From it he took a sealed envelope and laid it aside then another before sitting the briefcase back on the floor.

"Corporal Conley, I am authorized by the Commandant of the Marine Corps to bypass the exam and offer you a direct commission as a Warrant Officer Junior Grade. Do you accept the commission?"

James looked at Megan who was all grins and nodding her head. He looked at Crenshaw who just nodded once.

"Yes Sir, I do accept the commission."

The Colonel broke the seals on the envelopes and for the next thirty minutes James signed his discharge as an enlisted man and his reenlistment as a Warrant Officer Junior Grade. The Colonel admitted he had not seen the contents of the envelopes until he opened them, but his guidance was to give him the Warrant Officer Exam and if Jeff had passed the exam with Crenshaw grading the test, he was then to offer the promotion.

The Colonel swore James in then Crenshaw instructed James to gather up all his dress uniforms which would be taken to Quantico and used to insure he was properly fitted with Officer's uniforms. He was given two sets of Warrant Officer Junior Grade collar insignia for his digitals and a list of correspondence courses he could take on the computer to begin his new career. His Military Specialty Field was changed from Infantry to Intelligence.

After the dust had settled and they were once again alone in new quarters, Megan took James back to bed.

Just after midnight, three small drones came over the tree tops and were shot down by the Security detail. Two of them exploded upon impact with the ground. The third was recovered and examined. It had a RDX charge with a thermite mixture designed to cause a fire. It was figured that whoever had sent them was planning to damage the house and burn Megan and James alive.

They were informed the next day that the Colonel's original driver had taken a bribe from Sergeant Books, so Books could drive the Colonel that day. Books was talking but it was leading to a dead end. He said he had been approached by a reporter for the Washington Post and offered a thousand dollars if he could to get onto the Farm and locate the Red Tahoe. He said that the owner was being protected by the CIA for having knowledge of wrong doings so that the public would not become aware of corruption at the highest levels of government. The tracking device was in case they tried to move that person. He had been given information when the Colonel would be making a trip to interview this individual concerning corruption within the Marine Corps. Both drivers would be busted back to Corporal and sent out to Fleet Marine Corps units for the rest of their enlistments.

Conjecture

Dotty showed up on their doorstep three days later with a large folder and a concern about where the data originated from. She had the reports which Megan had requested in hand which had been delivered to the Dungeon by FedEx instead of being sent directly to Megan.

"Alright Megan, explain where this comes from and what you have gotten yourself into."

"Dotty, if you will remember, you hooked me up with Jake Grainger, so do you really have to ask those questions?"

"Damn it, he told me he had retired from those activities."

"He may have, but he told me he was only the messenger. I'm not sure what I can tell you but if the information is good, let's run with it."

"That's the problem, it is good, but we have no real traceability with it. Megan, this new Director has tried twice to shut us down, but congress will not let him. All he needs is something like this to point out that we are a loose cannon within his agency to convince the people who pay the bills that the money can be best spent elsewhere. What am I supposed to do? I can't spend all my time fighting him and get the job done."

"Dotty, if you want my resignation, please ask for it, I'll have it in your hands before you leave here. But this is not going to go away regardless what the Director wants, and someone needs to do something about it. It appears we have drugs being smuggled into South Korea using State Department controlled assets plus at least two of our local Korean Field Agents have turned up missing. We're involved whether the Director likes it or not."

"Ladies, may I interrupt for a moment?"

"Certainly James, go ahead." Dotty replied.

"We have been working hard trying to figure out who and why someone wants us dead. I think we have pretty much figured that part out but now we need to figure out why someone wants us dead."

"Wait. Did you just say why someone wants us dead after telling us we have figured out why someone wants us dead?" Megan asked.

"Let's look at it this way. Whoever is behind this wanted us dead to protect their operation, but we had no idea of said operation until recently. Granted it is still theory but I think we hit it on the head about the drug smuggling. Now we have to determine why it was so important we be killed to keep that operation quiet. These are still a few questions bothering me but give me a minute to explain."

Jeff went to a white board as spoke as he wrote.

"There are many ways to smuggle drugs into Korea, so why use State Department assets? Even after a couple weeks without interference from law enforcement in their smuggling operation, an attempt was still made to kill Megan. I can understand the attempt on my life since it happened so quickly after the warehouse incident which I might add did nothing to stop that shipment. Follow me so far?"

"Now what is the current political situation on the Korean Peninsula? Who would greatly benefit from a falling out between the South Korean Government and the U.S. Government if it was discovered that drugs were being shipped under the license and protection of the State Department?"

"Wait a minute James." Dotty interrupted. "If they wanted it known to disrupt dealings with us, why try to stop disclosure?"

"Because they are or were not ready for it to be discovered." He replied. "But let me back up for a minute."

James started writing on the board as he talked.

"The first attempt on Megan's life at the warehouse was planned otherwise no need to kill her driver. According to Megan's statement, the first man she killed told her in Japanese that they were going to rape her before killing her. Now why did he say that unless they had it planned to look a murder/rape crime. And with her looks, it could have taken weeks to get a proper identification on her."

"Now why did it take three weeks to attempt to kill her again in Korea? I think because whoever was operating on the peninsula did not have the contacts like the ones in Japan. It only took three days to attempt to kill me but not Megan. The hit on me could be written off as revenge since we have learned the man who tried to kill me in the hospital was related to one of the men who died in the warehouse. But the attempt on Megan used local talent of a dubious nature. Success meant she was out of the way; failure put a spotlight on her and would force the Agency to remove her from the peninsula. But this is where the waters begin to get muddy."

"How so James?" Dotty asked.

"What is the two most important events occurring to Megan prior to the third attempt on her life? First is being reassigned to the Dungeon. The Dungeon where cross-word puzzles and jig-saw puzzles are put together, so the world is a better place. If half of what I have been led to believe about the Dungeon is true, it is the most dangerous place in the world for people who intend to do harm to the world. Now add in Megan's meeting the man who created the Dungeon. This in a sense made Megan the most dangerous individual in the world simply because she is becoming obsessed with finding the answer to why someone wanted her dead."

"Wait a minute James." Interrupted Dotty. "Not five people knew the Gunner was at the Funhouse meeting Megan other than his wife."

"James, but I did not accessed that information source until you were becoming obsessed with finding the answers. Besides, the Gunner said he was asked to give the memory stick to me, he had not asked for the information."

James smiled at Megan. "Yes, the Gunner was asked to meet you and hand the memory stick over to you, but you did not access the stick until after the third attempt on you which happened to bring me back into the picture."

"No, wait a minute. Are you saying the Gunner is involved in this crazy scenario to kill Megan?" Dotty questioned.

"Yes and no. First of all, he only did what he was asked to do by someone within the shadows he once worked in. He even warned Megan about using the contacts on the stick. But even if he is out of the loop, I think he is involved in a way that is generous to Megan and myself."

"How so James?" Dotty once again asked.

James reached into his pocket and pulled out his gold coin.

"Dotty, how many of these have you seen?"

"Everyone on the original Dungeon team had one. He gave us one when we first formed the crew."

James looked at Dotty's driver, William setting on the couch out of the way.

"William, empty your pockets on the coffee table please.'

William put his coffee cup on the coffee table and just looked at James as Megan stood and brushed her shirt out of the way, placing her hand on her Sig. Dotty looked at Megan, then James and noticed he had put his hand on his pistol as he smiled at William. William chuckled then stretched his left leg out and very carefully reached into his pants pocket and removed an identical gold coin and held it up between his thumb and forefinger. James removed his hand from his pistol and Megan sat back down.

"William have you been informing on the activities of the Dungeon to the Gunner?" Dotty asked.

"No Dotty, Jake would not approve of such action on my part. His only request of me was to insure your safety and those who carried one of these coins. That is my only part in this except to learn and become part of the Dungeon crew. He recruited me to play this part and insured I was hired by the agency and would be assigned to the Dungeon after he retired. I do not work for him, only you. You are just going to have to take my word on that last part."

"Does Clifton have one of those coins?"

"Dotty, if he does he has not said anything to me."

Dotty turned her attention back to James.

"Continue please with your theory."

"Alright, where was I? Oh yes, from what I have observed watching Megan use the source of information, the source is vast and well back into the shadows. The people behind the information are powerful and wish to stay in the shadows. But what if one of them wished to have power beyond what they already have? What if they are using Megan to set the wheels in motion to create a breach in relationship between two allies? What if the Gunner suspected such things and is also using Megan to find the individual or individuals and bring them into the light of day before such events can take place. Before a war on the peninsula removes that source of democracy from the region?"

"James, how did you come up with such a conjecture?" William asked.

"Occam's Razor."

"Honey, that is a convoluted way of determining the answer." Megan put in.

"Yes doll, but what other formula do we have to use in this case? I can come up with no other way to make sense of the information we have available. I've eliminated all other practical answers and as obscure as this one is, it is the only one that makes sense."

"That means any information we receive from the shadows is now suspect." Dotty thought out loud.

"No Dotty, I don't think so. Whoever is behind this cannot risk discovery until it is time and tampering with evidence could be too risky. Granted, that is based on pure conjecture of course."

Dotty just sat and thought about what she had heard and the results if they did not find and stop the events from occurring.

"Jake once said that nature controls all we do. Nature cannot be rushed regardless of what we as humans attempt to do to control nature. He was always telling us to look for the pebble in the scene that did not belong there or was out of place. I had nearly forgotten those principles. Alright then. Megan do what you feel is necessary to find the answers. If you need anything the Agency can provide, let us know immediately."

"Our freedom." James spoke up.

"Excuse me James?"

"Dotty this may seem nice, but we are prisoners here. Captives of a system set up to protect us from harm, but we have no freedom here."

"Let me work on it."

"No Dotty." Megan's tone was strong. "We'll work on it, James and I, then we'll let you know how things turn out. Just tell Security to no longer prevent us from leaving the Farm. Do you know how to get ahold of Mark Lucas?"

Dotty sighed. "Yes I do. He is also retired except to contract services to the Farm from time to time."

109

"Good, then his coming to the Farm would seem routine. But what do you know about him?"

Dotty sent William out to warm up the car as she told the story of how she met Lucas and left nothing out to include the tossing of a traitor out the rear of a C-130. Once she was finished, she went to use the toilet and upon return, as Dotty was getting her coat on she asked an interesting question.

"How long have the two of you been lovers?"

"I fell in love with Megan the first time I saw her in Japan. But we have only shared a bed for three days."

Megan looked at James as he had finally spoken the words they had never exchanged even in the heights of passion.

"I'm not sure when I fell in love with James, but it was at least a month before we first made love. Does that answer your question Dotty?"

Dotty smiled. "Dave and I worked together for weeks before I gave myself to him. He had promised to marry me the very afternoon we were ambushed outside his apartment after work and after an hour of ruining his sheets. I killed the man who tried to kill us and have had no regrets. I hope what the two of you have survives this operation."

Dotty left them to return to Langley as they just stood in the living room, holding each other without speaking.

Name and Rank Please...

Master Gunnery Sergeant Crenshaw knocked on their door just before lunch the next day with clothing bags in his hands. His visit was short as he briefed them while walking to put the clothing bags out of the way. He quickly removed a large envelope from one of the bags, handing it to Megan as he was moving towards the door. His comments were precise and to the point. Megan was to have her hair cut short as she wore it during her schooling at the Farm. There was a female Marine uniform in the bags for her to wear tomorrow when they would be picked up for transfer off the Farm. Everything would be explained in the packet contained in the envelope.

Pack one bag for a week's stay as if they were going to take a vacation somewhere cold and mountainous. Their other belongs would be packed up and shipped to their final destination. Any intelligence data that could not be loaded to a memory stick stayed and would be brought with their other belongings. Be prepared to leave by no later than nine in the morning. Jeff was to leave his dress uniforms behind but could include his digitals in his bag.

James packed his seabag accordingly then helped Megan gather the intelligence information she wanted to take along. Her duffle was stuffed but manageable when they finished sorting through things, deciding what to take and what not to take. Megan had taken the time after lunch to go to the Farm's Barber Shop and have her hair cut into a Pixie cut. James had to stuff some paper in the Female Officer's Cover she was to wear due to the size difference her long hair to the Pixie cut made so it would properly fit. Her uniform was an Officer's Dress Greens with trousers and was outfitted with two rows of ribbons and Captain's bars.

The envelope contained their new Marine Identification cards and dog tags. Copies of orders directing them to Quantico and other items any Marine might have on them in case they were asked for by higher authority. Being a military brat, Megan figured she could pull the disguise off unless really pushed, so they both spent some time memorizing the information that might be needed is asked.

They checked their weapons, insuring they were clean and oiled, then went to bed early. Once again Megan awoke alone in bed but this time it was just after three in the morning. She pulled her long shirt over her body and went looking for James. He was standing on the patio once more looking out into the woods sipping on a cup of coffee. She poured herself one then went to stand beside him.

"What's on your mind Darling?"

"Baby, I'm worried about us. We are being used by unknown forces and it feels like we are getting ready to exchange one prison for another. One much more dangerous than the one we have here."

"I know James, I have those same feelings. But we decided to see this to the end and hopefully it will be the end that is best for us and the world."

"Yeah baby, I know. Megan, once this is all over with, what happens to us?"

"I hope nothing happens James. I love you as you well know."

"Then marry me. Marry me the first chance we have before this grows larger than we can manage."

"James my Love, I'll marry you right now if we had a minister to say the words."

"Thank you. Now finish your coffee and we'll go back to bed and try to get some more sleep before we start the next phase of this adventure."

Megan poured out her cup into a flower pot and pulled his head down and kissed him. They fell asleep in each other's arms, exhausted and very much in love.

At 0753, a Marine Corps Chevrolet Eight Passenger van pulled up to the house. The occupants quickly exited the vehicle with baggage and came to the house. The female was Asian and was as tall as Megan with some of her features. At a distance it would be hard to tell who was who. One of the males was built like James and in the dark, no one could tell the difference. The driver hustled them along helping get their luggage and weapons bags into the van and they left the other couple to stand as decoys for the next seventy-two hours. The driver had Megan lie down in the seat until they were over twenty-miles from the access road to the Farm. Other than basic instructions, he never spoke to them.

They were taken to Quantico and the guest housing where they placed in quarters normally reserved for full Colonels and above. As they walked into the house they were greeted by Master Sergeant (retired) Peters with a big smile and a hug for Megan. Once their driver had departed, Peters took them into the kitchen and sat at the table to talk.

"Okay kids, here is the game plan. For the next week, we will be at the Funhouse from 2000 hours until I'm satisfied with the nights shooting. We'll train with both handguns and your MP-5's. Now before you ask what else is being planned I cannot say, but nothing moves forward until I'm happy with the training. Mister Conley, I have no doubt about Megan's ability to pass quickly through the training, but you will determine how it progresses. I've seen your Marine Corps training records specifically your State Department training. Pay attention and you'll do fine."

"Thank you but what is the Funhouse?" James asked.

"It's an indoor shooting gallery where the FBI's Hostage Rescue Teams train for room clearing techniques. I know you had some of this type training while in the Embassy Protection Course, but this is more intensified. Megan has gone through it several times and the FBI has her listed as one of the top five shooters to ever go through it. So pay attention to Megan and my instructions and you'll be alright."

The rest of the meeting concerned why they were here and what freedoms they had now there were away from the Farm. Peters told them he had no idea and had not been informed of anything other than get them ready to defend themselves if things blew up. Again, he was more concerned about James than Megan but he stayed with the idea that James could come up to standards quickly. He left with many questions unanswered.

Just before noon, they were visited by Master Gunnery Sergeant Crenshaw who brought them some good news. They had the run of the base meaning the Officer's Club, theater and Base Exchange. He gave them both an American Express Money Card for use on base since their own debit/credit cards would leave a trail directly to them. Also, a rented Ford Focus was to be delivered later in the afternoon for them to use until further decision concerning their disposition was made.

They ate at the Officer's Club that evening then changed into civilian clothing for the Funhouse. Peters ran James through three rooms before he included Megan into the mix. He said the purpose was to make James familiar with the concept of the rooms even though each room would be different from the previous.

When the three started, Peters took the door with Megan then James following. The second room was opened by Megan and once it was cleared, she called cease fire and walked up to James, reached up grabbing an ear and pulled him down to her level.

"James Dear, calm the hell down! Stop rushing your shots, just take the shot as it comes and move on. We are not having a contest for who can put the most holes in the targets. Relax, it'll come in time. Okay Darling?"

"Yeah Baby, now let go of my ear before I spank you."

Peters laughed as Megan gave James a quick kiss as she released his ear. James straightened up, rubbing his ear as Megan moved aside.

"Take the door James!"

They took a total of fifteen rooms before Peters called it a night just before one in the morning. Megan and James spent the days resting for the nights training when they were not shopping at the Base Exchange or eating at the Officer's Club. When they trained with the MP-5's, James actually beat Megan's scores which surprised both Megan and Peters. James explained it later as he had trained with the MP-5 at Embassy School in such situations and understood his part better. His pistol scores improved as he adjusted from one weapon to another. He knew he'd never match Megan's scores, but he became confident in his own abilities.

On the fourth night, the FBI's armorers took the MP-5s and converted them to the silenced version. They also took the handguns and silenced them. It was awkward in handling the nose heavy pistols the first couple rooms but as they became use to them, they returned to a steady level as they passed from one room to another. At the end of the sixth nights training, Peters told them they were as ready as they could be as James had improved to the point he had leveled out nightly in his abilities.

When Megan finally asked Peters how much influence Jake Grainger had in this training, Peters only said that Jake was concerned about their ability to protect one another and that was all he was told. They parted company with James shaking Peters hand and Megan leaving a wet kiss on his cheek.

They had a couple days to themselves and on Friday evening, Megan put on a cocktail dress she found in a dress shop at the Base Exchange Mall and with James wearing his Officer's Dress Blues, they went to dinner then dancing at the Officer's Club. Over dinner, James presented Megan with an engagement ring he had purchased at the Exchange as Megan was dress shopping. She accepted the ring with tears in her eyes. During the evening, several Marine Officers followed protocol in asking for Megan's hand on the dance floor with James' approval. He granted each request as he watched Megan enjoy herself after such a long time being sequestered for so long at the Farm.

The night was fun for both of them as they danced until the Club closed, then went home and showered together before bed. Knowing they had no responsibilities the next day, they slept in but were awakened at 0800 by a phone call from Crenshaw. He told them he would be there at nine with VIP's and civilian clothing was acceptable. They showered again and ate a quick breakfast as they waited to see what was happening next.

Crenshaw brought three men with him, all in civilian clothing, but it was not hard to figure out they were senior military officers. The first part of the meeting was disturbing for James as they announced the plans for the two of them.

For the public record, James was being medically discharge from the Marine Corps on grounds the blow to his head in Japan had caused memory loss and reoccurring headaches making him unfit for further military service. He was being given a new last name, Simpson, and was being transferred to the U.S. Army as a Chief Warrant Officer Three with a complete service record showing he had enlisted in the Army at the age of eighteen. New uniforms were in the trunk of the sedan they had arrived in and he could keep his old Marine Uniforms as long as they were stored away, out of sight. Crenshaw offered to hold onto them until the mission was complete.

On Sunday, James would travel to Fort Benning and begin Parachute Training before meeting up with Megan at Fort Bragg. James did not like being separated from Megan, but she assured him things would be alright, just don't break anything while at Benning.

Megan was also given a new last name, Takahashi, and a service record showing her to be an Army Intelligence Officer at the rank of Captain. Further details of her assignment at Fort Bragg were not known except by the officer she was to report to there. She was not to have any contact with her parents off base and was to be very careful of contact with them on base. When Megan asked about how her disappearance was to be handled, she was told that last night her Passport was reported through Passport

Control as being processed onto a flight to Nigeria. The CIA was showing her reassigned to the Embassy there for duty.

Crenshaw explained that Dotty had filed a report stating they had hit a dead end with the examination of the reason for the assaults and later contracts on their lives and considered the project closed. Based upon the information they had, the contracts were revenge for the deaths of the gang members in the warehouse and since no further data was available, the theory that Megan and James had interrupted a hijacking based upon the reports by the Japanese Police, the case was closed. Transferring Megan to Nigeria was considered the safest way to protect her for the time being. Corporal Conley's medical discharge released him from further attachment.

They were given new cell phones under their new names and advised the GPS trackers had been disabled in them. They were to leave anything connecting them to the Marine Corps in the house and someone would collect it for storage after they had gone. Megan was given a partial set of uniforms and was told she would be outfitted at Bragg under the excuse that her uniforms were lost in transit by the airlines. She was also informed that her Tahoe had been removed from the Farm and completely repainted a medium Blue and had new California license plates on it under her new name. James would receive a Silver GMC Denali configured the same way while he was at Benning. The final thing they received were credentials showing they were Federal Agents and entitled to be armed at all times. They were told to use those licenses with caution.

James pulled Crenshaw off to the side before he left and made a request of him. At eighteen hundred hours that evening, James and Megan were married under their real names in the Base Chapel with Crenshaw and Peters as witnesses. The Chaplin told them he had a lazy Assistant and the marriage license would be lost for three months before being found and recorded for public knowledge.

After a short party at the Staff NCO Club as guests of Crenshaw and Peters, they returned to the house and exhausted themselves knowing it would be at least three weeks before they had another chance to make love.

A Sucker's Bet

Megan left for Fort Bragg an hour after James was taken away by Crenshaw to catch a flight to Columbus, Georgia and Fort Benning. She had taken her rings off and had them hanging from her new Army dog tags and traveled in civilian clothing. Megan was concerned about the flip phone she also carried having a GPS locator so she insured it was turned off and then wrapped in several times in aluminum foil to help block any signal. After some thought she did the same with the laptop before packing them both in a travel case separate from the rest of her things.

After she got checked into temporary quarters at Bragg she just sat and wondered how James was doing at Benning. She was tempted to call him but decided not too at this time. She also was tempted to call her folks but since officially she was supposed to be in Nigeria, thought if someone had their phones tapped, she would give her location away. Megan knew there had to be a manner of contact but had yet to figure it out. She had dinner at the Officer's Club then went to bed early and had a sweet, sensual dream of being with James.

James's day was not as easy as Megan's. Once checked into the Parachute School, he was assigned quarters and found himself rooming with a First Lieutenant who was also going to attend Jump School. The Lieutenant began to give James word and verse how they were to conduct themselves in quarters until James removed his Sig from the small of his back and placed it on his bed. James then tossed his Intelligence Credentials over to him as he began to unpack his things.

"Lieutenant, where did you go to school?"

"University of Colorado."

"Nice school. My Bachelors is from Purdue. I will respect your rank in and out of this room Sir, but do not push me. You will not like me if you do. You don't have enough time in service to dictate how I conduct myself in our quarters, but I will most certainly respect your privacy if you will respect mine."

"I will not be talked to that way Mister Simpson."

"Listen Lieutenant, less than twenty-four hours ago I was married to the woman of my dreams and now I am here sharing a room with another man instead of my bride. Thank God, she is also in service otherwise she may not have married me knowing I was leaving for this bullshit. I didn't ask to come here, I was ordered here for some God-awful reason unknown to me other than my next assignment is at Fort Bragg. So, try to relax and enjoy the ride. Now once I get my stuff put away, I'll buy you a beer at the club and maybe we can find a middle ground before this gets out of hand."

"What kind of Intelligence work do you do that requires you to carry a firearm?"

"The kind that you do not wish to know about and should not be asking about. You do not have a clearance high enough to have that information and respectfully Lieutenant, any loose tongue on your part about what I do for the Army will find you in dire straits. Am I clear on this Sir?"

"Perfectly clear Mister Simpson. I think I'll buy the first beer as a way to say I apologize for my earlier actions."

"No Lieutenant, I'll buy as I have already offered, and my name is James. I believe your name is Lieutenant, am I not correct?"

"Yes James, you are correct on the beer and my name."

James later showed the Lieutenant a photo of Megan taken with his cell phone in the dress she was married in. The Lieutenant was impressed and showed him a photo of his girlfriend that he planned to marry once she finished college at Texas A&M. They found the middle ground over two beers before calling it a night since training started at 0500 the next morning.

Megan checked in at the Base Personal Office and laughed to herself when she received her assignment. She was assigned to the John F. Kennedy Special Warfare School, position unknown and at the discretion of the School Commandant.

When she reported to the school, the first person to greet her was an old friend of her fathers who was now the Sergeant Major of the school. He greeted her as Captain Takahashi and took her to the commandant, another Green Beret she had known most of her life. Behind closed doors they told her she had an office assigned and to try to stay out of the way as much as possible until her partner reported in from Benning. Her father had been briefed about her new name and assignment and he had been told to attempt no contact with her unless it was face to face here at the school. Also, there was a computer set up in her office that was secure and could conduct business with the Agency as needed. It was encoded and the clone to it was in a place they only knew as the Dungeon whatever that was. Megan smiled and told the commandant she'd tell him about the Dungeon once this operation was complete.

Megan voiced a concern about the number of familiar faces she had already seen to which the Commandant told her any man that knew her from the days when she ran around the Teams with her father had been told to forget they every knew her and to treat her as an Army Captain they have just met. She was shown her office that carried the description of Intelligence Liaison with her new name on the door. The title made no sense to her and most people who wandered by it, but that did not stop men, especially single men from stopping by to say hello. Megan finally removed her wedding rings from her dog tags and put them on as a sign she was not available.

James called Megan nightly to let her know how his training was progressing, but they had agreed before he left to never mention the CIA or the operation they were involved in. Megan told him that her assignment had her writing or reviewing intelligence briefs for the Special Warfare School to use in training new men. He told her his Denali had arrived and he would leaving

Benning as soon as he could but he would be careful in driving up to Bragg.

Megan finally was able to meet with her parents in her office one evening after the administrative offices closed for the day. Her father asked about the rings on her finger as he wondered if they were part of her cover story. She showed them the photo of James she had on her phone and held nothing back about his background or what he was currently doing. They voiced their concern about what she was involved in, but she could not tell them anything which might lighten their concerns.

For James it was long days of hard training and short nights alone in bed. His roommate was injured early in the second week of training and left the school, leaving James alone at night without someone to talk to even though he could not talk about his actual assignment. Once they had come to terms about being roommates, James found him to be a decent type who admitted he was scared of the idea of parachuting but needed the wings to enhance his own career even if he never joined a parachute regiment. What James never told the Lieutenant was he had a fear of heights since childhood but the idea of jumping out of an airplane actually thrilled him.

For Megan, the time seemed to creep by with the clock in slow motion. She spent as much time as possible reading intelligence updates of the project, but nothing seemed to directly link the gang that assaulted her to any other aspect of the drug smuggling theory. The safety briefings were scheduled weeks in advance which they just happened to visit the warehouse at the right time to be alone. The juvenile gang problem was inconsistent with shipments departing from that specific warehouse. One troubling thing was the increase of drugs, specifically cocaine entering Korea.

Dotty sent a note to Megan that a five-man DEA team had been killed in Columbia during a raid on a cocaine processing location back in the jungle. The Dungeon crew was searching for a link between the drugs in Korea and the deaths of the DEA agents. As the drug influence was on the rise within the civilian population, there was no indication of problems within the South Korean military. A theory had evolved that there was an attempt to disrupt the South Korean government with the distraction of combating the rising drug problem within the country. Also, another Korean Field Agent had disappeared without a trace.

Megan missed James's ability to see through a problem. She attributed that talent to his chemical engineering education in that he was trained to look at the variables without becoming focused on a single aspect until he had deleted all other variables as non-viable to the problem. He was much better an analyst than she was, but she began dissecting the data so when James finally arrived, he would have less to wade through. She really missed his body next to hers at night.

She would from time to time accompany the Sergeant Major as he toured the training of new prospects hoping to be successful in completing the course and joining the Special Forces. She watched one group go through a live fire course and commented to the Sergeant Major she did not understand why so many men were having trouble with the course. This was overheard by the Special Forces Captain who was in charge of running the course. He challenged Megan to run the course. Megan told the Captain she would change uniforms and return within the hour and then had the Sergeant Major take her back to her Tahoe where she outfitted herself with her Sig and the M-4 Carbine that had been added to her equipment compartment of the Tahoe.

At the range she asked for a test fire to insure the optics on the M-4 were still aligned then started the course. She did not rush the course as she might have in the Funhouse but still took it at a greater speed than the trainees were taking. Megan swept the course with not only the instructors observing but also the trainees. As she was walking back to the start point, she saw the Sergeant Major collecting on a few bets that had been made to include what appeared to be a sizeable bet from the Captain. No one commented to her about her ability to shoot and move as she walked back to the HUMVEE, insured her weapons were clear and safe before getting into the vehicle. The Sergeant Major got in, handed her a fold of money and laughed at the situation.

Megan asked the Sergeant Major if he had said anything about who taught her to shoot and he said that he only told those who took his bet that he had faith in any woman sent to work at the school. She pocketed the money and cleaned her weapons when she got back to her office. Later in the afternoon, a couple of the instructors stopped by to ask her if she had time to show them her technique for running the course so they might copy it. She told them she would consider their request.

The day before James made his graduation parachute jump, Megan was notified by the Base Housing Officer that they had a house on base for her and her husband who they knew would be reporting within a few days. She went to the house, inspected it with the Housing Officer and accepted it partially furnished. When James arrived, they didn't waste time getting sweaty on the bed.

A Mission & A Team

James reported in and was assigned to the same office as Megan. They spent hours going over the data that had arrived while he was at Benning, but he agreed with the analyst that there was no direct connection. Megan had told him about running the tactical course and he agreed they probably should get as much time on it as possible since they could never be sure of where or what they might encounter a fight. They started taking an hour on the ranges daily with all of their weapons.

When they scheduled the tactical course, it seemed as if everyone not directly involved in training elsewhere were observing how they ran the course. The hours of running the Funhouse made hand communications easier for them as they moved through the course. After it was over, one of the men commented that they moved like a married couple on the dance floor. Megan smiled and announced that James was in fact her husband; they just decided to keep her maiden name until they left the Army.

Two weeks after James' return to Megan, they were sent to Fort Campbell to go through an abbreviated Air Assault Course to learn how to operate with helicopters. They both now wore Air Assault and Parachutist Wings on their uniforms. From time to time they went through training alongside of Special Forces troops to include extended field operations and force marches. The equipment they carried was light and not for extended operations but to accomplish the missions they were given. Megan never complained during the exercises, but James knew she was pushing herself hard in order to keep up and often at night at home he would massage her legs and back as she hurt from the loads she was having to deal with.

Megan was puzzled when they were ordered to Hubert down in Florida for training until they arrived and were greeted by Mark Lucas.

Mark Lucas had four men with him that he introduced to them at their new quarters in a hangar at the far end of the airfield. These men would be their operational team. Tomas Garcia was second generation Tex-Mex whose specialty was explosives. His background was Marine Recon. Howard Zimmerman was a former Air Force Para-Rescue who was their medical support and weapons. Chet Walker was another former Marine Recon who was a shooter, sniper trained. Jerome Conrad was a short, black man whose specialty was communications and was a former Navy Seal. Each man produced one of Grainger's gold Challenge Coins and each man had multiple combat tours in Afghanistan.

Training started in earnest in the vast, empty spaces of tropical, swampy terrain around Hubert. Lucas kept them busy for as many as twenty hours a day, building them into a team with Megan in command. From the very beginning the men knew she was CIA and not a trained combat officer but learned that she could anticipate much of what even experienced officers sometimes missed. Each man would offer advice from time to time which Megan would analyze then determine course of action. James had told her in private that a team such as Lucas was having her to build was outside the normal military parameters.

Megan learned her own weaknesses as quickly as she learned the strengths of the men she was to command. James learned how to move and operate as a team member beyond his normal training. None of the other men looked down on the inexperience of either Megan or James as they pulled together as a team. It was James's idea to make Jerome second in command of the team acknowledging his own lack of skills as they moved forward in training.

Communications was the key to every challenge they met as they moved from Hubert to Colorado Springs for mountain training. Their equipment was light, and their packs were set up for no longer than a twenty-four hour operation. It didn't take Megan long to understand whatever they ended up doing, it would be more of a hit and run operation. James worked hard at learning every aspect of the team dealing with communications and explosives. The team learned that Megan was just as good a shooter at any range and could match Chet with a sniper rifle.

Information from the Dungeon became sparse as nothing new was being discovered and they had hit a dead end. But eight weeks after the team was formed they ran a training operation which required a long climb up a mountain by ropes. At the objective they were met by the one person they never expected to meet. Jake Grainger. His briefing was short but not sweet.

"People, things have taken a dangerous step forward. Megan and James have a basic understanding of why you were put together, but you men just answered the call I put out. During the latter days of the Vietnam War, a syndicate was formed by wealthy and powerful men from all over the world with the idea that if the governments of the world could not protect its people and their way of life, then maybe they could by covert means. An interesting aspect of this syndicate was that even people who were considered enemies of our own country were involved as a means of protecting their own way of life. In other words, maintaining the status quo, but most importantly, preventing another world war."

"New members were recruited as old members died off in order to attempt to maintain a balance across the world. These people had access to intelligence and political intrigue far beyond many seasoned politicians. They have actually prevented the downfall of many governments to include our own many times over the decades. Three years ago, I was contacted by one of the members about the aspect of one of the members using the syndicate for wrong doing. I was given a list of things to look for and places to look without it being revealed to me who was involved in the syndicate."

"Megan and James stumbled into a covert plan to destabilize the Korean Peninsula in such a way that war would be inevitable. Megan first noticed things were wrong when two of her Korean Field Agents disappeared, only she had no idea the nature of their disappearance. But with her stumbling into the smuggling operation in Tokyo, the syndicate noticed an increase in activity within their own system."

"Contrary to history, the internet was created by the syndicate to keep track of operations and communicate with each other and those in their employee. The people who truly control the internet and the flow of information have been ruled out as possible suspects in the Korean disruption. Those people in turn were able to eliminate all but three members from the possible list of suspects. The traffic over the past six months keep pointing in one direction and it is that person you will go after soon."

"Now I'm sure the question going through each of your minds is why not give the information to the proper authorities and let them deal with it. Problem is at that point the syndicate would become public and in fact that information could cause many other problems almost as bad as war in the Far East. As far as why this specific individual desires a war is not as complex as it might seem. His companies are failing, and his wealth is being bled dry. A war would boost the economy and directly affect his business dealings, especially his military contracts."

Jake tossed a memory stick to Megan.

"On that stick you will find all the information you need to plan operations against this individual and his plans. Take him apart to the point he has to come out of his hole then take him down. As of twenty-four hours ago, he has a contract on his head. The syndicate is prepared to cover your actions as long as his demise is not public for all to see."

Jake paused before he continued.

"Megan, twelve hours ago you were killed in Nigeria by a car bomb in a public market. No one within the syndicate was responsible for the bombing, it was a true terrorist act, but it gave us a way to remove you from their thinking. Your parents have been informed of the deception and are secure with a Delta Force team protecting them."

128

"James, last week a homeless veteran was found dead in an alley in Omaha. He will be identified as being you and your mother will be briefed prior to the news release. This is not pleasant business people, but it has been considered that once your target feels he is no longer threatened by your presence, he will become a bit looser in his actions. You will find that within his psych profile, he has become paranoid about discovery as his plans move forward."

Tomas Garcia spoke up. "Gunner, how come you haven't gone after him?"

"Tomas, it is because not only myself, but my old team are being watched. They've all been warned and told to hold in position. Plus, I promised my wife I was done with running ops especially now that she is pregnant with our second child. And in case anyone is wondering, the tracking device placed on my Denali is somewhere over the Continental Divide on its way to Oregon with a load of John Deere tractors on a semi. Any other questions?"

"Good luck people." With that Jake walked over to a Jeep Wrangler and left the mountain and the people given the mission to remove the threat of war.

A Night Jump

From the mountain top, Megan's team was taken back to their quarters, packed up and moved again. This time they found themselves in an old ski lodge that had been replaced a few years earlier with a new, modern lodge. They were isolated once again but now had complete freedom of movement. The first thing they did upon arrival was for Jerome to rig sensors around the lodge, especially on the road leading to the lodge to give them some alert of visitors. Remote cameras were situated so if a sensor went off, the area could be looked at day or night to determine if the trespasser was human or animal. They received a lot of false sensor trips due to the deer and elk population in the area.

Megan did not access the memory stick until they were firmly located and secure then she began to dissect it with James's help. Their target was one Bruno Hochbauer, who was a reclusive billionaire who had fallen off the face of the earth as far as the public was concerned. The team was given six separate locations around the world that Hochbauer might be located but there was no confirmation of him being at any of them. Everyone except the security watch worked on the puzzle as James and Megan taught them how and what to look for across the internet.

Jerome set up a four-hour watch schedule on the security console which included Megan and James being considerate of their married status so they would have time together at night. For six days they scoured the internet for any mention of Hochbauer target without a single result. Since only one of the locations he may be hiding was located in the United States, they determined if they raided that location without result, it would give away their intentions and most likely cause him to advance his plans. Another aspect was that information developed by the syndicate said he now had a large protection detail of former military personal protecting him. The best number that could be determined was seventeen body guards but only their leader had any Special Operations experience. These were mercenaries paid to protect him.

They finally determined that first they needed to disrupt the drug flow from Columbia to their overseas market in a fashion to get Hochbauer's attention. Then disrupt his other business dealings in such a manner as not to give themselves away but require a more personal attention instead of his method of long range conversations to his onsite managers. How to do that was something they had to figure out. They knew the approximate area the underground drug processing facilities were located but in order to pin point them, they'd have to be on the ground. Information said there were three such facilities located in the mountainous region of Western Columbia, but they had to find them first. Once destroyed, they then needed to turn their attention to the businesses within the United States.

They formulated a plan and submitted it to Jake via a back door in the syndicate's network which was password protected. Two days later Jake responded with approval of the plan and a list of assets available and a time table for them to work under in Columbia. They had three days to locate each cocaine factory once the plan was initiated. Find the factories, set a target marker on each site and disappear without being detected or killed. Another asset would insure the destruction of the factories.

Megan broke the team into three, two-person teams with her teaming with Tomas while James teamed with Chet. Jerome and Howard made up the third team. With gear packed, they drove to Pueblo, Colorado and boarded a Lear Jet to take them to Belmopan, Belize where they transferred to an old C-47 Dakota cargo plane working under a false flag but actually part of the CIA's airlines. The target markers they were to use were in the plane at Pueblo and they studied the instructions thoroughly before once again reviewing their mission perimeters.

Thirty minutes out of their drop zone, they received their final go to target. They had changed from their civilian clothing after they boarded the C-47 and the men got a good view of Megan in panties and sports bra as she dressed for the mission. No one said a thing, but Tomas winked at James and gave him a thumbs up. They were going to drop in a common drop zone then fan out to their targets. Communications were encrypted and other than the maps they carried, no other item was on their bodies that might give away information. The maps were marked so that the only way to read them was with night vision goggles otherwise the marks remained invisible. The jump went better than planned as they all landed in a tight group within two hundred meters of each other.

They buried their chutes in the dense underbrush and separated moving to each location. Megan was taking the middle target and was on location before the others. She watched for thirty minutes before they spotted light streaming from an opened spider door showing them an entrance into the underground factory. Megan and Tomas had already spotted the two guards outside the factory and she had to smile as it was almost as easy as the exercise at Leonard Wood because they just sat and smoke cigarettes. Tomas was equipped with a silenced M-100 sniper rifle with night vision optics and covered Megan as she moved on the target. Megan had her silenced Sig P-250 in her hand as she moved around the guards and just back from the entrance they had seen, planted the marker and slowly moved away from the marker. It took her nearly two hours to make the complete trip in and out and once joined up with Tomas, they backed out of the area and headed for the rally point where the other teams would marry up with them before heading out of the area.

James and Chet did not locate their target until after Megan had given the code word on the radio she had completed her mission. Chet covered James as he moved on the target placing the marker then pulling out to a location to cover Chet as he moved to join him. Twice Chet had to freeze in location as a sentry passed by him lying in the underbrush. They gave the completion signal and moved to the rally point.

Jerome and Howard did not have as good luck as the others and were still searching for the entrances as the other two teams married up at the rally point. Finally, a guard opened the spider door giving them a central location of the factory. Jerome moved in and set the marker but had to kill a sentry on the way out.

Howard moved to assist Jerome and together they carried the body for nearly a kilometer before stashing it into the underbrush. As soon as they married up with the rest of the team, Megan retuned her radio and sent a single tone which activated the markers. From that point all they needed to do was clear the area.

Two hours before daylight they were sitting beside a dirt road waiting for their extraction. Twenty minutes later a U.S. Navy UH-60 Seahawk landed and extracted them to a Frigate off the coast of Columbia. As they were lifting off, three large fireballs could be seen in the night sky from the direction of the factories. A B-2 Stealth bomber had dropped two thousand-pound JDAM bombs on the infrared target markers.

On the Frigate they changed into the Navy's Blue and Grey work uniform then were flown by the Seahawk to a carrier further out to sea. From there the boarded a COD aircraft and were flown to San Diego. At San Diego they boarded the Lear Jet that had taken them to Belize for the return flight back to Colorado. The only contact they had with Naval personal on any ship was with the ship's Captain and the aircraft personal transporting them from point to point. When asked who those folks were, the Captain's only said Delta Force personal and to cease with the questions. Both ships would remain at sea until the team's mission was complete and all ships personal were cautioned not to mention their presence on the ships or face charges.

Once back in Colorado, the team stood down for twenty-four hours before planning the next phase of their mission. Even the security watch was only scheduled after dark since someone was always up during the day to check any sensor alarm.

Sabotage

For the next week, the team examined blue prints of various plants that were vital to Hochbauer's business. Shut down the plants in quick order and he had to come out of hiding. It would also help if the Chief Operating Officer (COO) of each plant was taken out of the picture. They received some unexpected help when one union threatened to strike for more benefits.

With James help they identified key locations to sabotage which would shut the plants down for days if not weeks without the risk of injuring or killing employees at the targeted plant. Once more they wrote up the plan and sent it into the internet along with a list of needed materials. Forty-eight hours later, Mark Lucas showed up with the items requested in a FedEx marked van. They had a total of seven plants targeted and once again they broke into three teams with Megan and James teaming up as advised by the rest of the team.

Tomas built the charges as estimated required for each location and made sure every team member knew how to handle them, attached them to the area they wanted to damage and how to handle the timers. Every item could be found in any hardware store except for the explosives which could be found in any rock quarry for blasting rock. Tomas demonstrated the timers using a twelve-volt light bulb which flashed on when the timer hit zero. All they had to do now was get into position, survey the target and set the explosives.

Each member of the team now carried U.S. Marshall identification with business cards stating they were part of the Marshall's Felon Recovery Division. Each carried a name different than their real name. They traveled to Colorado Springs and at the Air Force Academy, they changed vehicles to GMC Denali's with U.S. Government plates and U.S. Marshall registration. Government credit cards for use as needed and a complete set of identification for each individual. Each member of the team quickly realized there were some powerful people backing their operation even if they would never be known to them much less the public unless they failed.

The union went on strike as the targets were being surveyed and security at each plant tested by the teams. Just after dark, eight days after leaving Colorado, the first charges were set. None of the targets were closer than two hours apart so the first charges were set to coincide with what they projected so they would all blow close to the same time. Chet and Howard had three targets and Howard planted one charge as Chet planted another then Chet picked Howard up and moved to the third target together.

Jerome and Tomas accomplished their mission but were stopped by the California Highway Patrol for speeding. Tomas was driving and flashed his Marshall's identification and told the trooper they were on their way to Barstow where they had a report of a felon being spotted. The trooper asked them to use their emergency lights while traveling and let them go. Tomas turned on the lights in the grill and back window before he pulled back onto the highway and soon left the trooper far behind.

By daylight the network news was a blaze with news of sabotage by the striking union which the union denied. Each team drove straight through to the lodge, changing drivers at each fuel stop. Howard and Chet were delayed enroute when they came upon a wreck between a semi and a car. Chet put his Para-Rescue training to work helping the victims until Paramedics could get on the scene.

During the return to the lodge, events were occurring that were being dealt with by other, unknown sources. One COO was injured in a car accident and taken to the hospital. Even though he stated he was not hurt in the wreck, a CT scan showed he had internal injuries and was being held in the hospital to insure his health. The actual scan was of another person who had been killed in a car wreck three days earlier, and the patient data had been changed to show it as the COO's scan. The accident was staged by barely known Hollywood stunt man who would later find himself with plenty of work as long as he kept his mouth shut about the accident.

Another COO came down with food poisoning hours before the first charge went off. He had a habit of ordering Chinese food on the very night the teams had chosen to set the charges. He would be out of action for days.

The third COO was removed from his home by civilian authorities as part of a child porn sting. This was actually a legitimate arrest, but the local police had been asked by a Federal Agency to hold off making the arrest until they had other evidence for other crimes to be mentioned later. From the time the police received the notice, it only took them less than thirty minutes to have the man in custody.

Fate offered a hand in taking out a fourth COO when a rock thrown by a striker hit him in the head knocking him unconscious. The team had estimated they only needed to take three of the COO's out of the picture to bring the target out into the open. The fourth just added gravy to the stew they were brewing. Now all they had to do was wait for their target to make a move.

Weird Ideas Might Work

The team set watching the news around the clock as the media blamed the unions for the sabotage and the unions blamed the corporation for trying to the break the unions by sabotaging their own plants. The Board of Directors were holding long sessions trying to keep the corporation alive as their stock kept falling on the Dow Jones and NASDAQ. They were calling for Hochbauer to return to the board room since he was the majority stockholder and they needed not only his voice but his signature.

Intelligence reports were coming in a steady stream from the syndicate. A shipment of cocaine was seized on the Tokyo docks and several gang members killed and over a dozen arrested at the end of a long investigation by the Japanese Police. In Korea, A Korean Marine detachment boarded a Philippine registered vessel to seize several hundred pounds of cocaine and other drugs before they could be offloaded at the Inchon docks. Reports out of Columbia said the Columbian Federal Police had determined the explosions that destroyed the cocaine factories were caused by carelessness by workers in those factories. Millions of dollars of drugs had been destroyed or seized over a week's period. The word was also out that the drug cartels wanted their money for the lost product destroyed in the factories.

Hochbauer finally surfaced at his corporate headquarters in Milwaukee to give his voice to the repairs of the plants and union demands. The team held in place since his home in the Milwaukie area was in a crowded residential area as they waited to see where he went from there. Hochbauer's appearance on television shocked the nation as he seemed sickly and underweight as photos of his last public appearance was compared to him now. Forty-eight hours later he moved to his retreat in Idaho which was two thousand acres of wilderness surrounding a near fortress with eight foot high stone walls surrounding the mansion. A private helicopter pad located inside the walls gave him a quick get-away if needed. Within hours of his arrival in Idaho, satellite photos began to arrive of the retreat.

James woke up a few minutes after two in the morning alone in bed. He knew Megan did not have the watch at that time and wondered what she was up too. He pulled on a pair of sweat pants and went looking for her. Megan was standing in front of the sixty-inch television they were using as a monitor staring at the overhead of the retreat. She was only wearing her favorite tie-dyed oversized t-shirt. James walked to stand by the security monitors and gave Chet a questioning look. Chet just shrugged his shoulders and turned back to also watch Megan. James walked up to Megan and gently took her in his arms, pulling her back into him. She gave his arms a gentle pat and just sighed.

"What's wrong baby?"

"James, this is impossible with only six of us. We have over five hundred meters of open ground between the tree line and the wall with at least seventeen Mercs that we know of inside the walls. An unknown floor plan of the mansion adds to the problem and we have no idea how many people in the house will resist an assault on the mansion. I'm lost here James and don't know what to do."

James gently turned her around to look her in the eyes.

"Megan, you are not in this alone. Please come back to bed and get some rest then tomorrow we'll start looking for weaknesses in the target. Please come to bed, I have gotten used to you being there at night."

Megan smiled at him then rose up on her toes to kiss him.

"Hey. You two get a room." Chet jokingly commented.

"We've got a room and yes, I'll go back to it with my husband." Megan laughed.

Back in their room they just cuddled up together and went back to sleep. Megan's sleep was fitful as she kept seeing James covered in blood lying on a floor. They woke at six and James fixed breakfast for the whole crew as Megan returned to the

138

overhead view of the target. Over breakfast, Megan mentioned they needed a better view, one from ground level. Time was the problem in they had no idea how long the target would stay in Idaho plus anything like drones flying over the retreat might spook him.

It was Chet who came up with an idea to get things rolling.

"Let's see if the folks behind all of this can shut down communications into and out of the fortress. Cell phones, internet, even any satellite communications to include television. Then we take a trick from the Japanese snipers of World War Two."

"Sniper in the trees?" Tomas asked.

"Yeah, but unlike those snipers, we rig a slide line before a single shot is taken. One or two well placed shots, slide down the line out of the line of fire and move to another location. Megan shoots as well as I do and Jerome is a fair shot. We use fifties and cause as much damage to material and personal as we can. One maybe two well placed shots will take out the helo on the pad and if we can get line of sight, the power transfer from the generator to the house. Anyone out in the open is fair game."

"If we can get six of the M107A1 Barrett's on short notice, we can raise hell for two or three minutes with the security personal along with the material we can get to. The range is less than one thousand yards and even I should be able to hit the mansion at that range." James put in.

"Okay, we climb the trees how?" Tomas asked.

"Pole climbing spikes. Not hard to use going up but using them coming down can be a bitch without training. But with a line down, no need. Without a man on the ground, a slide line would be near impossible to rig so we'll have to repel down. Rig the rifle to a drop line, let it go and follow it down. From that point it's just a matter of sniping on them from time to time to keep them off balance." James answered the question.

"No." Megan spoke up. "We'll only go with three Barrett's unless we cannot get three M240's for suppression. After the snipers do their work the others can fire into the compound where they see the security folks gathering to counterstrike. We'll have to watch out for the possibility of counter-sniper snipers but once we are on the ground and after fifty to one hundred rounds sprayed into the compound from each 240, they can follow us to the ground and shift as a team. Any comments?"

"While we are generating a wish list, a forty-millimeter grenade launcher or two would be nice." Howard commented. "Preferably the M32."

"Okay, what do we do once the shooting stops? Six of us against how many we don't dispatch in the first ten minutes with them behind a wall and us spread out all over God's creation. I like the base idea but what happens next?" Jerome put into the discussion.

The discussion went on for over an hour with all coming up with the same conclusion, there were not enough of them to make any manner of assault on the mansion, much less the walls. Megan wrote up the wish list and background of the base plan to include the conclusions they had made about assaulting the retreat. They did not even have the personal to keep them bottled up inside for more than twelve hours, if that long, once they decided to make a break out of the compound.

An hour later Megan's flip-top cell phone buzzed causing everyone in the room to stop talking. Megan opened the phone and smiled as she read the message.

"Hold what you have. Events rushing forward in our favor. Wish list approved if needed. Stand by for further orders. JJG."

Megan showed each man the message and it was Howard who asked what JJG meant. Megan told the group it was Jake's initial, John Jacob Grainger. Everyone relaxed, checked their gear and that evening the team gave Megan and James privacy as they used the hot tub on the back deck of the lodge before bed.

140

For four days they sat at the lodge with Jerome taking charge of keeping the team in shape with exercises and short runs up and down the old ski slope trails. The news media moved on to other stories as the union and the corporation came together in settling the strike. The syndicate sent daily reports via their network to the team keeping them apprised of Hochbauer's situation. All communications into and out of the retreat compound had been severed except for a single channel used by the syndicate to let the target know he had failed.

The night security watch maintained Megan's flip-phone in case a message was sent during the night so response would be quicker than having it wake her up and try to read it while half asleep. One the fifth night it buzzed during Tomas's watch. He had a small air horn like used at football games and just held the button down on it as rooms opened and the team came running to the living room. Tomas handed the phone to Megan.

"Stand To, stand by for pickup at 0700. Digitals required. Combat load. JJG."

The team had a complete set of Marine digitals including rank for use if needed and this morning it appeared to be needed. Megan and Howard prepared breakfast for the team as the others dressed then got themselves ready. All of their gear was laid out in the living room as Jerome ran through a checklist to insure nothing was left behind that might be needed. Camelback bladders were checked to insure water down to pencils for making notes. They were ready to go by 0600. All they had to do was wait.

At 0655 they were spread out on the front porch, completely saddled up and ready to leave when they heard the sounds of a large helicopter approaching. Within a minute a Marine CH-53E Super Sea Stallion pop up over the tree line and make a circle confirming a landing zone. Jerome rushed out into the middle of the old parking lot and acted as ground guide to bring the big helicopter in safely. One thing every member of the team noticed were the big Browning M-2 machineguns hanging out the side ports of the helicopter. This was serious business and the Marines were armed for it.

The ramp was coming down as the big helicopter made a soft landing on the parking lot. The Marine crewman manning the pedestal mounted M-2 Browning on the ramp waved them to the bird and they left the porch at a run with Jerome moving from in front towards the rear. Boarding the aircraft, they found it was already occupied with Marines. Megan was handed a set of earphones as she found a seat at the rear of the cargo bay and put them on over her soft cover. The bird was lifting as the ramp was coming up and a Marine across the way from her signaled with his hand.

"Captain Takahashi?" Came over the headset.

"Correct. Who are you and who is in command?"

"I'm Lieutenant Bowers and you are in command Captain."

"Brief me on your orders Lieutenant."

"Yes Ma'am. We are in support of a raid to be conducted by a team of U.S. Marshalls against a terrorist group holding VIP for ransom. There are two other platoons moving up to meet with us at the target location via helicopters at this time. You are in overall command of the strike force if the Marshall's get into any trouble they cannot handle."

Megan looked at the Marines around her noticing many of them were looking at her.

"Lieutenant, your men look like they are ready to go. Any problem with them taking orders from a split-tail while under fire?"

Bowers face took on a shocked look at Megan calling herself a split-tail. A derogatory term used to describe female Marines. Then he laughed.

142

"No Ma'am. Word is this is not your first dance and you have notches on your K-Bar. I just don't think the men were ready for someone as attractive as you are to have such a reputation. Pardon my forwardness Captain."

"I'm not sure the reputation is earned, but you can ask my husband later about it. He's sitting next to me." She pointed at James.

Megan removed her seat belt and moved to the middle of the floor as she waved Bowers to meet her. Bowers had a map of the compound out to the tree line and they laid it out on the flooring and went over it. The pilot in command of the helicopter came back as she devised landing strategy for her Marine assets. Her platoon would land on the road leading to the main gate and spread out along the tree line with the other two platoons landing equal distance apart and taking up the same positions. If need be, they would close the ring on the compound with the squad machineguns providing supporting and suppressive fires as needed. The big CH-53's could orbit as long as possible to also provide fires from their door guns if needed. The pilot made his notes then went forward to the cockpit and contacted the other helicopters advising them of the plan of action.

When she asked about the helicopter inside the compound, the Marine pilot told her that they had been advised that the Air Force had a couple of F-16's overhead with instructions to shoot the helicopter down if it attempted to take off and the people inside the compound had been so advise. The pilot chuckled when he said they received word that the Falcon pilots buzzed the compound at tree top level to make sure their presence was noticed.

Megan's worst fear was that the Mercs in the compound had a manner of knocking one or more of the big helicopters out of the sky before they could land and discharge their human cargo. Bowers had pointed out his radio operator and told Megan that he would be by her side and had all the call signs necessary. All she had to do was tell him what she wanted, he'd deal with it.

143

Five minutes out from the compound, the pilot gave a warning and Bowers stood up and indicated to his men to lock and load. At a minute out, everyone stood and readied themselves for the rush into the open. Bowers had briefed his squad leaders and platoon sergeant on what he wanted them to do so all they had to do now was wait for the ramp to drop and step out into the daylight.

Megan exited the aircraft and went to the middle of the road and just stood there looking at the compound's gates. Her team surrounded her, and James very roughly pushed her down to her knees. Except for the sound of the helicopters it was deathly quiet. Megan watched as the other two birds lifted out of their LZ's and in a dance the three big helicopters began to orbit the compound, maintaining distance as they gained altitude. Her radio operator advised her all elements were in position and standing by.

Howard tapped her on the shoulder and pointed behind them. Vehicles were moving up the road towards them with their flashing emergency lights. They stopped about twenty yards behind Megan's group and the Marshall's began to dismount the vehicles with a tall Black U.S. Marshall in the lead. Megan stifled a laugh as Mark Lucas approached them.

"Captain Takahashi, my name is Powers. We ready to do this?"

"This is your dance Mister Powers, lead on; we are just here in case the house band plays a sour note."

Lucas/Powers motioned for one of the vehicles to move forward and he climbed on the running board as it passed. They drove within roughly one hundred meters of the gates and stopped. A voice was heard echoing from the vehicles loud speaker system advising all inside to exit the compound with hands in the air and leave all manner of weapons inside the compound. It was less than a minute later that the gates opened, and men began to exit with hands in the air and walked down the road pass the vehicle towards the Marines.

Bowers moved forward with a squad and stopped the line of men which now included a couple women wearing maid uniforms as each person was searched then cuffed with plastic ties. Megan moved forward and checked the females for weapons before they were also cuffed as the people were being moved behind the Marines lines with another squad watching them.

According to the man who said he was the caretaker of the compound, Hochbauer and his personal assistant were still inside the mansion. Megan signaled for her team to gather up on her and they began the move towards the gates. The last man to exit the gates had been the head of security and claimed no one else was in the compound except the two she really wanted in cuffs.

Just as they entered the gates, first one then a second shot rang out from inside the house. Megan never thought as she called out for James and Chet to take the door. Room by room they cleared the house with Megan standing in the living room with the radio operator waiting. Tomas sang out they found them in a bathroom. Hochbauer was in the bathtub with a bullet in his brain and his assistant on the floor with a pistol in his hand and a bullet in his brain.

Megan called for Bowers to bring the rest of his platoon up and once there, she had them completely search the mansion and compound for anyone that night be hiding that the security chief had not noticed or mentioned. As this was taking place, she had the prisoners separated into two groups, the Mercs and the civilians then had them placed on separate helicopters and taken out of the area to a location Lucas gave her.

Once Bowers reported the compound secure, she ordered the Marines to stand down and go on fifty percent watch until finally determination could be made of their status. The big helicopters landed at their platoons and shut down with the door gunner facing the compound alert in case of need.

This was all anticlimactic to Megan as she kept wondering why the PA had killed himself and his employer. She turned to find James, but he was not to be seen. She walked back to the

145

living room when a small explosion erupted from the second floor of the mansion. Marines sprinted up the wide staircase with Megan mixed in with them. They found a Marine laying against the hallway wall slumped over and James on the floor about halfway out a room door. Megan rushed to him and she saw what her nightmares had seen. James covered in blood. A Corpsman had come up the stairs in the initial rush and the call for another Corpsman rang out through the mansion.

Megan dropped too her knees and picked James's head up and moved a leg under him as she held him. He groaned at the movement and she knew he was still alive. Howard came to a sliding stop beside them with the team's aid bag and began to work on James as Megan held him. Soon Howard had him stripped from the waist up, checking for wounds then cut his pants apart to bandage several large cuts and other wounds to his legs. Most of the blood on his face came from cuts, but his Gargoyle wrap around glasses had protected his eyes.

As this was happening, Megan heard her radio operator call for litters and to wind up the remaining helicopter for medivac use. A Marine appeared with a fire extinguisher and put out the small fire in the room where the explosion occurred and once Howard deemed it safe to move James, they moved him further into the hall. The Corpsman working on the downed Marine determined he had only had his bell rung hard, but tagged him for evacuation.

James became conscious as Megan held him while Howard started an IV in him. He looked up at her then spoke.

"Baby that was the PA's office. We didn't touch anything, that bomb must have been on a timer. Sorry about this Megan, I really am."

"James my dear, do not give me any bullshit. Just stay with me. Howard is working hard to keep you with us so help him all you can. Besides your child will need a father in a few months."

"You're pregnant?"

"I think so, I missed my last period."

"Well I'll be damned."

"Hey, you two can set up house later, we need to get him moved and out of here." Howard injected.

Megan wiped the blood from his face and gave him a soft kiss before surrendering him to Howard and the Marines who had brought a litter up for him. Megan held his IV up and she walked beside him, holding his hand all the way to the helicopter that had moved to as close to the gates as its blades would allow. Jerome caught her as she was going up the ramp with James and reminded her she was in command and had to remain behind. Howard remained with James as they flew to Boise for emergency medical treatment. Lucas had quickly told Howard to report them as injured in a training accident and to say no more than that. The helicopter crew stowed their Browning's away during the flight and Howard had removed his weapons for when they left the aircraft for the emergency rooms.

A team of forensic FBI agents appeared on the scene an hour later and Megan told the agent in charge she wanted a complete DNA profile on the PA, Harris, along with detailed examination for possible cosmetic surgery to his face. An Osprey arrived as the helicopters returned and the Marines returned to their home base as the Osprey took the team back to Colorado.

Jake was waiting for them when they landed and briefed them on James's status. Jake smiled when Megan also asked about the condition of the Marine hurt with James telling her he had a concussion but would be back humping the hills soon. James' body armor had protected him from major injury, but he had also suffered a concussion along with the cuts and puncture wounds to his legs and arms. Jake also informed Megan that the contract on her and James was now invalid as word was spreading that the payer for the contract was now dead and unable to fulfill the terms of the contract. He also told her that the people watching his old team had been rounded up and it was discovered they were only locals hired to keep an eye on the team and to notify Hochbauer's PA if the team moved to marry up.

The team was ordered to stand down and relax until Howard could catch up and the syndicate could determine the next step. Everyone stayed out of Megan's way as they waited for Howard to return with first hand news concerning James.

Howard arrived two days later with Mark Lucas. He briefed the team on James's status advising them James would be transferred to the hospital at Fort Carson as soon as the attending physician deemed him ready to travel. Howard then turned on Megan telling her to change her clothes they were taking her to Colorado Springs and the Air Force Academy to be checked out. When she started to complain, the entire team took sides with Howard as Lucas just stood aside and laughed.

The Air Force Doctors were surprised when their dispensary filled with Marines escorting a female Marine officer and explained that she might be expecting and wanted to insure that if she was pregnant, things were alright with the baby. Two hours later the Doctor returned to advise the men that Megan was in fact approximately six weeks pregnant and the baby was doing fine. When he asked which of them was the father, Jerome told him with a straight face that her husband had been blown up a few days earlier, but would recover in a few weeks to resume his husbandly duties. The Doctor, who was a Major, just walked away shaking his head and mumbling something about Marines being insane.

Megan accepted her new condition and position with the team as they returned to the Lodge. All their equipment was inventoried, cleaned and packed for storage. Tomas gathered all of the explosives and detonators taking them out to a shed for temporary storage until they could be picked up for disposition. Ammunition was inventoried and then disbursed amongst the team. James gear was handled by Jerome and Megan as they waited for orders.

Lucas returned three days later and handed each man a large envelope containing airline tickets and money. He took the men away leaving Megan alone at the lodge. That afternoon, Dotty arrived with Dave, William and Clifton with her new orders.

"Megan, you have a decision to make. What you will do from this point on?"

"What about James? What are his options?"

"James has only two options. He is still under an enlistment contract with the Marine Corps and his lateral transfer to the Army is valid if he wishes to continue there. But he will have to serve out his contract."

"Dotty, I'm pregnant and would like to wait until I talk to James before I make any decision concerning the rest of my life."

"Yes, Megan I understand. Tomorrow James will be transferred to the Army's Hospital on Fort Bragg. You will return to Bragg to your assignment there as before until James is able to return to duty. There are no longer any restrictions on your movements, so you can visit your parents anytime you desire. You'll have to maintain your cover identification so not to cause too much confusion or questions. Is this alright with you?"

"Perfectly Dotty, thank you."

When they left, William and Clifton were driving James's Denali back to North Carolina with both his Marine and Army uniforms and other personal items. Megan left the next day after an older couple Dotty had told her about arrived to take over the caretaker duties for the lodge.

Megan once again had her CIA credentials in her possession along with the Army Identification needed to assume her duties at the JFK Special Warfare School. She returned to the house they had on base and her duties the next morning since she had arrived too late in the evening to visit James in the hospital. The next morning as she was busy reviewing a training intelligence report to be handed out to the students, there was a knock on her door. It was the Colonel, the School's Commandant, was standing there holding a cup of coffee.

"You have a free minute Captain?"

"Always for you Colonel, please come in."

"Megan, I understand Mister Simpson is in the hospital with some interesting injuries. Take whatever time you need away from the office to see him. We both know this assignment is nonsense anyway, but I have to say you have done a great job for us."

"Thank you, Sir. It might be a temporary assignment, but I would feel ashamed if I didn't try to accomplish something while marking time."

"Your father would say the same thing. Word is you are just as dangerous as he was in tight places."

"I'm not sure where you may have heard that Sir, but let's keep that between us."

"Not a problem Megan. Now I understand your career is up in the air for now. Ever consider staying in uniform?"

"It has crossed my mind. James has an enlistment contract to fulfill and until I talk to him, I'm not sure what I want to do. Plus, I'm expecting now so I must consider our child."

"Yes, I have been informed of your pregnancy. Which reminds me, your field schedule is now purely limited to observer status, am I clear on that Captain?"

"Perfectly clear Colonel and thank you. Is there anything else Sir?"

"Yes, get out of here and go visit your parents before that crazy Indian comes here and tries to remove my tonsils for keeping you away from your mother. Then go see your husband before he crawls out of the hospital looking for you. The Sergeant Major saw him yesterday and told him you would be reporting for duty today."

Megan laughed and put the papers aside that were lying on the center of her desk. She stood, picked up her uniform cap and followed the Colonel out the door. Her father seemed to take her being pregnant without much excitement, but her mother was all over her insuring she was comfortable in her chair and that she was taking care of herself. Her brothers were in school, but she promised to come see them later. Her parents followed her to the hospital as they wanted to see James and make sure he had what he needed.

James was sitting up in a chair when Megan entered his room with her parents following. He had bandages on his face and one leg was straight out covered in bandages. He smiled a crooked smile as he tried to stand up. Megan made him sit back down as she kissed him around his bandages.

"Baby, I'm sorry, but the docs say I'm going to have a few scars on this ugly mug. I hope you can tolerate me with them."

"James darling, the only thing that matters is you are alive, so put such things out of your mind."

James smiled again then looked to her parents.

"Master Sergeant Wagner, Mrs. Wagner, please sit down. It is good to see you again."

"James, you either call me Horace or Dad, I'm retired and you calling me Master Sergeant sounds like you are preparing to give me orders."

Her parents stayed for about thirty minutes before leaving them alone. Megan told her about the Colonel suggesting she stay in the Army and asked Jeff's opinion. He told her that the Sergeant Major had explained his options during his visit yesterday and he thought they needed to relax for a bit before making a final

151

decision. James told her that he was told it would be a month before he would probably be released from the hospital and once in the privacy of their home, they could work out the pros and cons of her staying in service.

James went home within the month predicted and was on thirty days convalescence leave. Megan took thirty days leave to be with him as he continued to exercise and run to regain the damaged muscle mass from the injuries and surgery. James was very vocal in that Megan being careful with the exercise in order not to hurt the baby. They both returned to duty together and on the first Friday formation after their return, he was called forward and presented with a Purple Heart for injuries suffered in a classified operation. No one ever asked him about the operation since it was not unusual for those within the Special Forces community. James was also award his Green Beret even though he had not been through the course.

A New Assignment

Megan was six months pregnant when James came home late in the evening from field exercise with an 'A' team that was still in the developing stage. He found that Megan was not alone even though there were no cars parked in front of their house. Jake was sitting on a kitchen chair with Dotty and Dave sitting on the couch with Dotty holding their new daughter. Mark Lucas was sitting on another kitchen chair as Megan was in her padded arm chair in civilian clothes.

Sitting in the living room chairs for guests were two individuals who were wearing suits that James knew did not come off the rack at Sears. The elder of the two gentlemen spoke up.

"Warrant Officer Conley, would you mind putting your shower off until we have a chance to talk to you and your lovely wife?"

"No one has called me Conley in over a year. Yes, I'll wait on my shower if you can put up with my stench. It has been a hard day Sir."

"James Honey, please calm down, they have something to offer we need to listen to."

To everyone in the room James's tone did not seem upset but Megan knew her husband very well.

"Sorry Baby, it has been a rough day. Sorry gentlemen, what have you got for us?"

James sat down in his recliner and waited for the boot to drop. Dotty started the discussion.

"James, Megan, the results of the DNA tests on Harris, the PA who killed himself, says he was Korean. Most likely North Korean since it appears he had extensive cosmetic surgery to make him look Caucasian. From what could be recovered from his office, he was manipulating his employer's business dealings

153

without his knowledge. He was the one who put the contract out on the pair of you."

"So is the status quo once again in balance?" Megan asked.

"Yes, it is thanks to the two of you." Jake responded to the question.

"Gunner, everything I did was to protect Megan the only way I knew how. If anyone thinks that was wrong of me to place her over the rest of the world, well, you can guess my next comment."

"No Mister Conley, I don't think it was wrong of you because in protecting Megan you were working to protect the rest of us without realizing it." The younger of the two gentlemen responded. "Which brings us to the reason we are here tonight. First, we have something for you as, if you will, a reward for a job well done." He removed a thick brown letter size envelope from his coat pocket. "Here is the title to the lodge and the surrounding land where you stayed to launch your operations from. It comes with no strings attached. Being that you are both still in government service, a monetary reward for services rendered could attract unwanted attention. Please accept the property with our thanks."

James looked at Megan who nodded an affirmative to him. He then reached over and accepted the envelope then handed it to Megan without opening the envelope.

"You said first. What's next?"

"We'd like the two of you to stay here at JFK and be available when or if needed to take on certain assignments much like the last one for your country."

"No." Megan softly spoke. "No, I will not stay here. I married James Conley not James Simpson and our child will not be born improperly named. I want to carry my husband's name to work daily even if I have to resign from the Agency."

"You called it Gunner. She has spoken as you said she would." The older gentleman spoke.

Megan tossed the envelope on the coffee table. "I am aware what our combined pay is with my Agency pay and James's Warrant pay plus the subsidies to him from the Agency. Even at that level of pay, we cannot afford the property taxes on a place like the Lodge. So, take it back."

"No Mrs. Conley, you keep it." Again the younger man spoke. "The property taxes are covered for the next one hundred years and the couple acting as caretakers are on our payroll. To be honest here, we had hoped that you would also use the lodge as a staging area for any operations you feel you can accept."

"Well gentlemen my wife echoes my own feelings. I will admit I enjoy and respect working with the Special Forces folks as I did today, but I am a Marine. I would like to return to the Corps even if it means I return as a Corporal and Megan as a dependent wife. But please make the decision soon as Megan needs to establish a home wherever we go and prepare for our child's birth."

"Megan," Dotty spoke up. "You are now on medical leave with pay until the baby is born. We'll work on the details required afterwards."

The older man stood then the younger man as Jake also stood. Dave took the baby as Dotty stood. The older man looked a Jake.

"Take care of it Gunner." Then he walked to James and shook his hand as James stood up. The younger man followed suit as they both also shook Megan's hand then moved to the door. Dotty went to Megan, bent over and kissed her on the cheek as Dave shook James hand. Mark Lucas shook both of the hands without having spoken during his time there. Jake was the last to

155

act. He pulled another envelope from inside his jacket and added it to the title to the Lodge.

"Gunner Conley, you will report to Quantico in two weeks. Get your shit together and uniforms in proper order." He shook James hand then moved to Megan, bent over and gave her a kiss on her cheek. "Major Conley, see if you can keep him in line."

With that Jake moved to the door, opened it and preceded the others out the door. James went to the door and saw a limousine now parked in front of the house which Jake and the two unknown men entered. He saw Dotty and Dave get into the back seat of a Denali with Clifton holding the door who nodded to him before getting into the front and them driving off.

James returned to the coffee table and picked up the envelope Jake had dropped on it and opened it, taking the papers out. There were orders for Chief Gunnery Warrant Officer Four James L. Conley, USMC, along with orders for Major Megan Ann Conley, USMC, to report to Quantico, Virginia. Megan smiled at the orders and gave her hand to James so he could help her up from her chair. She told him to get cleaned up while she fixed him something for dinner. He asked for ham and eggs as he left to get cleaned up.

While she was getting everything set up in the kitchen, the flip-phone she had carried for the past six months went off. She looked at it as it had not once buzzed since Idaho. She flipped it open and keyed up the message and laughed. It was simple in context.

"Standing By For Orders."

Act II

Mexico

Megan was backed into the corner of a small alcove watching down the alley way for sentries or anyone else moving about at this time of night. She had entered this spot barely three minutes before and killed the sentry standing in the dark, hiding from his compatriots. As she had eased around the corner into this location using her night vision goggles she saw the sentry and she quickly reacted by placing a bullet into his brain. He had jerked back against the wall behind him and she pushed against his body as he slumped to the ground ending up looking as he was squatting in the dark. When she looked for his weapon she found it leaning against the wall then another look at the body she found out why. He had his manhood in his hand and it appeared to be still erect in death. Megan gently moved the AK-47 to the ground and turned to watch her assigned area for intruders while her team was busy with their assignments.

They were thirty-five kilometers South of Vera Cruz, Mexico and fifteen kilometers from the Gulf Coast at a villa that had been taken over by ISIS as a terrorist training center. Their mission was simple in concept; capture or kill the American ISIS terrorist that had set up this camp and bring him back to the United States or leave a corpse behind. This was where simple stopped and complex began. The target was the product of the short marriage between a Mexican immigrant father and an African-American mother who had converted to Islam when he was eighteen then managed to find his way to Syria and fought with the ISIS for two years. His knowledge of Spanish was the reason he was in Mexico recruiting, for public knowledge, men who would cross the border into the United States and assist in the return of Texas and New Mexico to Mexico where certain Mexicans believed they belonged.

It was deathly quiet as Megan's team moved into position. Chet Walker had taken a location where he could cover the teams egress with his silenced M-100, AR-10 based sniper rifle. Megan's husband, James Conley was positioned with a FN M-249 SAW to also cover their egress in case things turned nasty. Jerome Conrad, the team's Number Two was leading the entry team composed of Howard Zimmerman, the team Medic who was going to sedate the target for movement and anyone who might be with him to keep them quiet as they removed him from the villa. Tomas Garcia, their explosive expert would set charges as they egressed to blow the villa and confuse any attempts to quickly locate the missing terrorist as they made their way to the coast and their way out of Mexico.

Megan's ear bug crackled. Two set, meaning Jerome and team were ready to enter. Five set was Chet letting everyone know he was in position and ready. Three set was James also announcing he was ready. Megan keyed her radio and whispered into her boom microphone; One set. Go.

Jerome's team was entering through the patio doors of the room which intelligence said their target was using as his bedroom and Megan was listening for any sound that might give them away. There was no sound except for the sound of a rat scurrying across the cobblestone of the alley. The seconds ticked by feeling like hours until a single code word came over the radio; Bingo. Jerome had their target under control and now she had to wait out the next code words so she could leave her hide. Noise to her left alerted her to the possibility of an intruder and she just leaned back into the small alcove she was standing in. The lizard striped uniform she was wearing blended in perfectly with the darkness, breaking up her outline in the darkness. She keyed her radio and whispered; Hold. Everyone stopped what they were doing and waited until either the emergency code went out or to continue as planned.

Megan waited as the noise came closer until first a head then the body of another sentry stepped into the edge of the alcove and never felt the bullet enter his brain through his left eye socket. Megan caught his body as it was falling to the ground, trying to prevent a racket caused by the body and weapon rattling on the cobblestone. He was a heavy man and even as good a shape she was, it was a struggle to get him down quietly. Megan swore to herself to work out harder once back at Quantico. She took a quick look both ways down the alley then gave the code; continue.

She just squatted in the alcove watching and waiting until she heard Jerome give the code they were clear of the villa. About a minute later she heard Tomas call clear and she began to move up the alley to meet up with the team at their rally point. Just before she gained the corner to the road she had to cross, Megan heard Chet call hold. She was down on one knee when she heard a wet splat then a body hitting the cobblestone. Move it One came the call and she moved across the road seeing a body to her right of the man Chet had just killed. Across the road and into the vegetation she moved quickly as James called clear letting Chet know he was moving. Chet gave a thirty count then gave the call clear as he was also moving to the rally point.

At this stage of the operation, timing was critical as the charges Tomas had placed would detonate at 0200 hours which was seven minutes away as they gathered at the rally point. No time was wasted as they joined up and continued towards their hidden transportation to the coast. Tomas had point with Megan behind him, then Jerome and Howard carrying their burden with Chet then James bringing up the trail.

They had gone barely four hundred meters when the villa erupted in flames. The team never looked back to admire their work as they closed on their transportation. A few minutes after the villa went up in flames, a violent secondary explosion occurred when the ammunition and explosives stored there detonated. Soon they came to the old International pickup truck they had earlier stolen and tossed their captive in the back and boarded the truck with Tomas driving and Megan in the front beside him. Tomas had pulled the fuse to the vehicles lights when they had stashed it and was driving using his night vision goggles.

Megan pulled her GPS from her vest and watched it as they moved to the coast. Five kilometers away from their pick up point she broke radio silence to give the code word for the Zodiac boat crew to move in and pick them up. The code was acknowledged. Just before Tomas crossed the inter-coastal highway, he stopped and waited as they watched two fire trucks pass moving towards the main road to the villa. This was figured to be the main danger point as they crossed the highway and headed for the beach.

Tomas pulled the truck behind a sand dune they had spotted when they first came ashore nearly twenty-four hours earlier and the team moved to the beached Zodiac. Megan had given the final code word as they crossed the highway so the boat crew would know they would soon be arriving. The team crossed the beach in file with James watching their rear. When everyone had boarded the Zodiac and as it slowly pulled back off the beach under power, she called James to join them. He was waist deep in the water when he placed his SAW in the boat and climbed aboard. Jim Tillman, their coxswain, was a former Navy Seal and expertly maneuvered the craft out to sea where a sixty-foot luxury yacht was waiting for them.

From the moment Megan had given the code for the Zodiac to move in and pick them up, the yacht's captain had been watching the yacht's surface radar for unwanted guests. As long as he was silent, the way to the yacht was clear. Eight miles out from the coast they rendezvoused with the yacht. The Zodiac pulled alongside the lowered swimming platform at the rear of the yacht. Howard and Chet moved onto the platform and the prisoner was passed to them then onto the rear deck as the rest of the team moved onto the yacht while passing weapons and other gear until the only thing left was Jim and the Zodiac. Jim pulled the igniters on a half-dozen small charges around the boat and climbed onto the platform as he pushed the Zodiac away with his foot. The big engines of the yacht come alive and the yacht began to pull away from the Zodiac as the charges detonated, ripping the craft apart and the weight of the outboard motor pulling it down into a watery grave.

The first priority once aboard the yacht was to clean their weapons to insure no salt water had invaded vital parts to cause corrosion. They did this while drinking coffee and running through the mission with comments of places they could have worked the angles better. Megan mentioned the two sentries she had to kill but did not comment on what the first one had been doing as he died. Jim and his boat partner, Kevin Short, just sat back and listened to informal mission debrief. They did mention that when the villa went up it could be seen out into the Gulf but not as bright as they would have imagined. Tomas laughed and told them it was because of the way he had set the charges to take the building down, not blow it up. Tomas was making a living when away from the team blowing up buildings for a Dallas demolition company.

After the weapons and other gear was cleaned and stored away, the team cycled through the two showers aboard the yacht, cleaning the sweat and grime from their bodies. It was warm as the sun came up and Megan changed into a bikini and lay out of the fore deck of the yacht as part of their camouflage. She was enjoying the rocking of the yacht as a Navy UH-60 Seahawk flew over then circled the yacht as the yacht reduced speed then came to a stop. The Seahawk approached the rear of the yacht while lowering a cable. Jerome caught the cable and attached it to the rescue basket the prisoner had been strapped into, and then steadied it as the Seahawk pulled it up. Once the basket was secure inside the Seahawk, it nosed down and flew over Megan as the helicopter's crew chief waved at her. Megan waved back then pulled the floppy hat she had in hand over her face and closed her eyes. Except for getting home, mission complete.

The team set foot back into the United State in Galveston where the team broke up and headed to their homes knowing their bank accounts would be credited with payment for services rendered by unknown sources. James and Megan drove home stopping for one night before moving on. They wanted to get home to their three-year old daughter, Melissa who was being watched by Megan's mother in their absence.

Memories

The after-action report for this operation took Megan nearly two hours to type up and submit via her coded laptop. As always, she noted the lack of concise intelligence for the target site, but she had learned like many operators that if you think you have all the intelligence you need, then you missed something. James had reviewed the report before he headed out to do a survey of one of the training sites as was part of their cover at Quantico. This brought back memories for Megan of those first months.

A week before they left Fort Bragg for Quantico, Mark Lucas appeared at their doorstep with a brief case full of trouble. It was trouble because Jeff rebelled at the items presented him. It was the ribbon bar which James was to wear on his Marine uniforms that upset James in that it contained a Silver Star and a Bronze Star with "V" plus two Purple Hearts. Lucas, who was now their liaison to the syndicate, explained each medal and the paperwork behind them. The Silver Star was for the action against the Korean intrusion as was the Bronze Star for his actions in the warehouse. The Purple Heart's also reflected the two injuries received, the head wound in the warehouse and the bomb in the mansion. He had both Iraq and Afghanistan Campaign medals to validate the medals without people questioning them. Megan convinced James he had earned the actual medals and to please accept his place as a hero whether he felt like one or not.

Megan's own ribbons were impressive for a woman with a Bronze Star with the "V" for Valor and a Legion of Merit plus the Afghanistan Campaign Ribbon. She also was awarded a Purple Heart for the leg wound she had suffered during the ambush in Seoul. Both had Parachutist Wings on the uniforms with Megan's being the Silver Army style wings while James were the Gold Navy wings. James also had a Combat Diver's Badge which Mark explained he would eventually earn before the year was out.

The move to Quantico did not go as they envisioned as when they contacted the Base Housing Office there were no quarter's available for them. Dotty got word about the housing problem and within an hour she contacted Megan about a house thirty minutes from the main gate. When Megan asked the rent, she was told to just move in and relax. Furniture not included. They stayed in a motel for the first two days as they shopped for furniture and kitchen appliances. The only problem James had with the house was that it had four bedrooms plus the master bedroom and a four-car garage. Megan figured they could almost play volleyball in the living room. James figured that with both of their housing allowances, they might fill the house within a year if they found some good buys. They found out the house was built as a display home and had not sold until an unknown buyer purchased it for them to use while at Quantico. It was decided that if anyone asked, the house belonged to James's uncle who had purchased it as an investment and was letting them use it until property values returned or they were able to get into base housing.

Reporting into the Base Personal Office was nearly as bad as the housing situation since they had no idea what to do with them other than to hand over a very large sealed envelope from Headquarters Marine Corps. A note attached to the envelope stated they were to report to a specific building and that was all the information they had to work with. Arriving at the building they first saw it was small, almost as if it had built as a storage building but it had new signs posted and this caused Megan to laugh until James realized the joke. The building was now the Office of Training Analysis, a play on the CIA's Planning Analysis. Signs designation parking spaces had two specific signs up with one stating Major M.A. Conley and the other CGWO4 J.L. Conley. One was shown reserved for the secretary that had a vehicle parked in it.

Inside they met their secretary who happened to be Kathy from the Dungeon crew. Dotty had asked her to assist and she accepted the job since she was single and jokingly admitted at Quantico there were hundreds of muscular, single men available. James took exception to Kathy's assignment until Kathy swore that she had not been put into this position to keep Langley informed of their actions. Megan was officially still working for the CIA and James was still seconded to the Agency, so her assignment meant someone with the proper security clearances were taking care of their daily paperwork. Megan let Kathy know that she understood the situation but if a single word of what they were up too found its way to Dotty without their knowledge, she was gone.

They broke the seal on the large envelope and found their mission statement and guidelines for the day to day work to cover their assignment to Quantico. There was also an envelope addressed to the Commanding General, Marine Corps Base, Quantico. Kathy placed a call to Base Headquarters and was finally put through to the Chief of Staff who granted them an appointment that afternoon to present their credentials. This is where James was glad Megan was in command as the meeting with the Chief of Staff did not start off well.

They were sitting in the Chief of Staff's outer office five minutes before their appointment time. Ten minutes after their appointment time they were finally granted entrance to his office. Whether he intended for them to sit in his outer office that long or not did not matter to Megan as she only wished to complete this part of her mission and get off her feet as the baby was raising hell inside of her. When she stopped in front of his desk and reported in the Colonel suffered several shocks as he looked at her and James.

The first shock was that this officer standing before him was very pregnant. Then the ribbons on her chest showed her to be above the average female officer he was familiar with since very few he knew wore Parachutist wings plus expert rifle and pistol badges. A Legion of Merit, a Bronze Star plus a Purple Heart spoke volumes about this officer. Then the Gunnery Warrant Officer standing beside her was even more impressive. The scars on the Gunner's face spoke of a nasty business verifying the two Purple Hearts he wore. This was a warrior without any doubt. His final shock was when he noticed both of them wore identical name plates. Conley.

He finally found his voice.

"Excuse me Major, please be seated." He semi-stood and then motioned to the chair to his left.

"Thank you Sir, but we are here to see the General Sir."

"Major I believe I can handle whatever you need to see the General about. What do you need?"

Megan raised the envelope she had in her left hand up so the Colonel could see it.

"This is for the General Sir."

"Well, give it to me; I'll see he gets it."

"With all due respect Colonel, my orders are to personally hand it to the General and to no one else Sir."

The Colonel looked at Megan then James.

"Gunner, would you please step out and close the door behind you while I have a discussion with the Major."

"Sorry Colonel, he'll stay. Besides being my husband, he is also my Executive Officer Sir."

"Are you being insolent Major?"

"No Sir, but I will follow my orders as given to me Sir."

"Fine, I order you to give me the envelope and retire from my office. This meeting is over."

"Sorry Sir, you do not have either the rank or authority to countermand my orders. Good day Sir."

Megan and James did an about face and started out of his office.

"Stop where you are! Where do you think you are going?"

"Back to my office Colonel until the General has time to see me, Sir."

"I'll have you up on charges of Insubordination if you take another step. Who is your commanding officer?"

"Yes, Major Dear, who is our commanding officer?"

"Yes, that would be interesting to know Gunner." A voice came from the door. The Colonel stood up as they turned back to the door to see the Base Commander standing in it.

"Major, I expected you this morning. Problems?"

"My fault General." James spoke up. "The monster was giving the Major fits all night, so I took her to Sick Bay this morning to be checked up, Sir."

"And how is the monster doing Major?"

"Fine General, just fine. It seems the little monster does not like Thai food Sir." Megan responded.

The General laughed.

"Step into my office Major and let's leave Colonel Brockhurst to his next appointment."

Once in the General's office, Megan presented the envelope to him then accepted the chair he had offered.

"Major Conley, I had my aide call your office to see when you could make your presence here and found out you had an appointment with Colonel Brockhurst at 1345. He kept you waiting, didn't he?"

"Yes Sir, he did."

"I overheard most of that conversation Major, watch your step. I know who you really are but I'm the only one, and if you push the wrong buttons too hard you will embarrass some very powerful people. Do you understand me?"

"Yes Sir, sorry Sir, but the Colonel made it too easy."

166

The General just waved it off as he read through the documents in the envelope. He sat one aside then pressed his intercom and summoned Colonel Brockhurst to his office. When the Colonel arrived, the General just held the one paper up for him to take as he read others. Brockhurst read the document then stood looking at Megan waiting for the next shoe to drop. The General finished reading and sat the documents on his desk letter side down so Brockhurst could not see them before speaking.

"Colonel Brockhurst, does that memorandum answer your earlier question about who the Major reports to?"

"Yes Sir it does. Thank you Sir."

"Colonel, we are to give them what support is necessary for them to accomplish their mission here at Quantico, so I think two range capable vehicles with radios will be necessary in their mission. See to it today and have communications assign call signs for the Major and the Gunner."

"I'll see to it right now Sir." As he started to leave the General spoke one more time.

"And Colonel Brockhurst, when a junior officer states you that do not have the authority to countermand an order they have received, then I'd accept it at face value. You can always tear their ears off later if proven wrong."

"Yes Sir."

After the Colonel left the office Jeff spoke up.

"General is the Colonel going to be a problem Sir?"

"No, but others might be until they understand your mission here and I'm speaking of your Marine mission. I do not want to know what else you are up to otherwise." He tapped the papers upside down on his desk. "These are my orders, instructions on how to deal with your other mission. I'm going to ask this one question and I expect an honest answer and it will be the only time I shall ask such a question. Answer if you feel you can."

"Go ahead Sir."

"Some months back there was a Special Ops mission in Columbia using Naval assists to extract the team. I understand one of the team members was a woman, a very attractive Asian woman. I take it that woman, was you?"

"General, I don't know where you heard that piece of information, but I would advise them to keep quiet about things they know nothing about. But a night jump into the jungle can be very interesting, right James?"

"Very interesting Megan my love."

"You two knock off the act." The General laughed. He reached into his pocket and tossed a Gold coin onto the desk. "Does this tell you anything Megan? May I call you Megan?"

"Certainly, you may General and I'll refer to you as General if that is alright with you."

The General laughed then told them to get out of his office he had work to do.

That afternoon two GMC 4X4 pickups were delivery with radios for use by the Office of Training Analysis.

Setting up shop was not as easy as anyone had estimated since the only guidelines they had to work with came in their mission statement provided by Headquarters, Marine Corps. They were to survey all training Marine Corps wide and make suggestions for improvement to the local commands, but were not required to submit those suggestions to Corps Headquarters. This did in fact create a circle the wagons attitude amongst the training command on Quantico since the memorandum they had received did not clarify the difference between suggestions and instructions to implement changes.

Units were to provide copies of their training schedules, so Megan and James could plan their days as they waited for the next mission. The week after they opened shop, they received a bit of a surprise when a Corporal entered the offices with orders in hand to report for duty. He had been ordered to assume duties as Megan's driver by the Chief of Staff. Megan accepted the orders and dismissed the Corporal to the outer office until needed. She then went into the coded system, entered his personal information and waited for the reply. It took less than an hour. James told Megan he'd deal with the situation and called him into his office.

"Corporal Jenkins, pull up a chair, we need to talk."

"Yes Sir. I just got here so I don't think I've done anything wrong Gunner."

"First of all, Staff Sergeant, whose idea was it for you to be a Corporal instead of your actual rank?"

Jeff got the reaction he was expecting. Jenkins looked as if he was about to make a break for the door.

"Sir, I don't know what you are talking about."

"Bullshit Marine." James leaned forward and handed a printout to Jenkins over his desk. Jenkins took it and seemed to pale even more than he already had.

There, on the printout was not only a photo but a brief breakdown of his service record to include dates of promotions. Nothing on the printout showed where the information originated from or how it was obtained. The most damaging piece of information was Jenkins Military Specialty and duty assignment prior to reporting as Megan's driver. Jenkins was an investigator from the Norfolk Provost Marshall's Office, Criminal Investigation Division.

"What now Gunner?"

"Word and verse Staff Sergeant. What were your instructions and who gave them to you, and if you hedge on them

169

one iota, I'll let my wife have a go at you and she is nowhere near as polite as I am."

"I was directed here to report to the Colonel Brockhurst, the Chief of Staff, who advised me that something was not right with the positioning of this office and its staff. He wanted to know what game you and your wife was running against the Marine Corps, and who was behind it if possible. He did make one statement that rings true though and that was to insure the Major did not come to any harm during her pregnancy by going into the field to check on training if that was what you people would actually be doing. Otherwise I was to keep my eyes open for anything that might be out of line."

"Staff Sergeant, you have thirty minutes to be in proper uniform or I will personally escort your ass to the brig. You will not have any contact with the Chief of Staff or anyone in his office during that time frame."

"Pardon me Gunner, but do you have the authority to have me brigged?"

"Do you care to find out Staff Sergeant?"

"No Sir, I'll just go out to my car Sir, I have my proper rank insignia in the trunk Sir."

James walked across the hall to Megan's office and just looked at her as she smiled. "Unless he trips over himself and is injured, we'll keep him until the brat is born so I don't have to worry about you being out and about alone."

"Yes, dear." Was all Megan said.

An hour later, Megan was sitting in the Base Commanders office witnessing one of the nastiest ass chewing's she had ever seen as Colonel Brockhurst stood centered on the General's desk at attention as the General was leaning over the desk in his face.

Six weeks later Megan was standing behind the firing line observing the men of the Infantry Officer's Basic Course qualify

170

on the rifle range when she suffered a hard pain in her abdomen which nearly doubled her over. Jenkins was never far from her and reached out to keep her from falling over as he yelled for one of the Corpsman who attended the ranges. They had the field ambulance move to her position and carefully loaded her into the back as the pain seemed to get worse. Megan told the Corpsman her due date was still two weeks away as he cut her maternity trousers off her so he could examine her as the Range Safety Officer first called for a Medivac Helicopter then called cease fire on the range.

Jenkins called James on his cell phone to advise him of her status and as they were talking the call over the Range Control Net for a Medivac was heard on James's truck radio. James was seven miles away observing a Warrant Officer class run through the Obstacle Course.

It was nearly ten minutes later the cry of a baby could be heard issuing forth from the back of the ambulance as Melissa Sue Conley entered the world. Aloud cheer arose from the range as she was greeted by the Marines present.

Continuing to March

James was raised without a father and turned into a very attentive one for his own child to the point Megan had to chide him about coddling the baby. He did bring his mother out from Omaha to visit her new granddaughter for a week after Megan and Melissa came home from the hospital. The doctors could not figure out why she gave birth in such a rapid order especially since this was her first child, but both the baby and Megan were in good health after the event.

The Base Commander was in conference when he got the word of Melissa being born on the rifle range. He laughed and sent his aide to purchase a dozen roses to be delivered to Megan once she was admitted into the base hospital. Mother and child became celebrities for a short time due to the nature of Melissa's birth. Megan had to call the General in order to keep her photo out of the Base paper or the local off base papers.

Megan took thirty days maternity leave before reporting back to work. Two weeks after the birth, the doctors cleared Megan to return to exercising so she could get back in shape. During this time, James took Jenkins with him on various inspection tours to Camp Lejeune or Parris Island. Jenkins was intrigued at what he witnessed from an observers view of training. At first Jenkins was critical of several points of the Infantry training he observed until James reminded him that even though all Marines were Infantry in base form, Jenkins had spent his career as a Military Policeman, therefore his view was tainted by that experience, and to look for the little things that might need improving or even deleting. Once he got over that hurdle, he seemed to recognize the importance of the things he at first felt was either unnecessary or overdone.

Jenkins stayed with the office until Megan was back a month before being shipped out to Okinawa which upset Kathy since they had quietly been spending late nights together. Soon after Jenkins departed, Colonel Brockhurst retired after learning he was passed over for promotion to General and was replaced with an officer that seemed to ignore the presence of the Office of Training Analysis.

Melissa was six months old when they received a request for consideration of a mission into the Balkans. Megan looked hard at the mission perimeters then handed it off to James who spent hours going over the intelligence before deciding that they would not take the mission and wrote a concise rejection report of why it was not practical for their team to undertake the mission. Two months later Dotty visited them with a report that an Agency Black Ops team attempted the mission and failed. Many of the reasons for failure were listed in James's report.

Nine months after Melissa's entry into the world, the team, minus Megan went into Central Bolivia, near Cochabamba and rescued the son of a wealthy German industrialist who had been kidnapped while touring with university group. Jim Tillman and Kevin Short had been added to the team for this mission. Megan protested being left out of the mission, but the team overruled her as they felt she was still not up to her previous physical standards even though she was working out daily to return to her former physical condition. Melissa was with Megan's parents as she sat at the lodge waiting for the team to return from the mission.

This mission was a success with no casualties on either side as once the team moved into position, they quickly learned the young man had not been kidnapped but was keeping company with another young man. The team brought out both men plus a young couple that was also on location. It seemed the victim wanted the ransom money so he and his lover could start a new life without the interference of his father. Megan filed a scathing report back through the syndicates system concerning the value of intelligence since the young man's sexual preference had not been mentioned in the package the team had received. The team members were all well paid for this mission including Megan and James. They in turn, placed the money into a college fund for Melissa.

Megan was observing live fire at the Sniper School when the senior NCO, a Master Gunnery Sergeant, took exception to her observing the activities. He was aware of her official duties, but thought since no women had entered the course, she was not the one to report on the school. Megan excused herself with a smile and returned to her office but not to file a report but to pick up her Accuracy International .338 Lapua that had been built by one of Delta's Forces armorers. James walked in as she was checking to make sure she had plenty of custom loaded ammunition and asked what she was preparing to do with the rifle. She told him and he laughed then told her he would spot for her.

When they arrived at the range, the Master Gunnery Sergeant at first thought it was James who was going to shoot the course until James handed the rifle to Megan and just smiled at the Master Gunny. The line was cleared and Megan took the center line position and set up with James lying beside her with his spotting scope. Twenty rounds later the Master Gunny called cease fire. Megan rolled away from her rifle and looked up the Master Gunny with a smile as the Marines observing were quietly talking amongst themselves.

"Major Conley who taught you to shoot?"

"My father did Master Gunny. Long before I got my first period."

That comment got a laugh from the men observing the firing.

"May I see that rifle Major?"

Megan motioned for him to pick the rifle up and as he examined it, he noticed it was not a standard Accuracy International built rifle.

"Who rebuilt this rifle Major?"

"Master Sergeant Dedmon."

"Bill Dedmon?"

"Yes Master Gunny, Wild Bill Dedmon."

"Who might your father be Major?"

"Master Sergeant Horace Wagner retired."

"You're Crazy Horse Wagner's daughter?"

"Yes Master Gunny I am, and he does not like that nickname nor do I."

"Sorry Major, I'll not make that mistake twice and please accept my apologies for my earlier comments concerning your observation of our instruction."

Megan stood and looked at the Master Gunny with a sly grin on her face.

"Master Gunny let's be honest here, I sandbagged you. But just because a person has to squat to take a piss does not mean they are not capable of certain aspects of the world where the participants normally stand to take the same piss. Am I clear on that subject Master Gunnery Sergeant?"

"Crystal clear Major. Now if you and the Gunner would clear the line, we'll get back to our training today."

A week later James went to Norfolk as part of his cover to review the training the Marines stationed there were undergoing especially the FAST Company Marines. The reality was that a SEAL Team was running him through an accelerated version of the Combat Diver's Course.

James was two miles off the Virginia coast taking his final Combat Driver's swim towards the beach when Megan's flip-phone buzzed a simple message: Stand-by. In turn she hit the forward command and the message was sent to the entire team's cell phones including James's. No one would be moving towards the Lodge until Megan gave the 'go' order but this was for them to be prepared in case she decided to take the next step in preparation for a mission.

Regardless of how long he was gone, James always brought something home to Melissa and this time was certainly no different. He brought her a stuffed bear wearing a frogman's outfit complete with tiny air tanks. But even as much as she wanted to stay up and play with Daddy, James made her go to bed at her scheduled time then he and Megan went over the information she had received that afternoon before they went to bed.

Ten kilometers south of the town of Rivercess Liberia, an Al Qaida affiliated group had set up a smuggling operation bringing weapons into the country. They were also smuggling diamonds and possibly young girls out of the country. Reports said the girls were for sex slaves or prostitution slaves to fund Al Qaida operations. Three days later they dropped Melissa off at her parents and headed for the Lodge. Neither Melissa nor James liked the idea of being separated again so soon after him returning home.

The team was at the Lodge by the time Megan and James arrived and no time was lost going through the intelligence being provided daily as they worked out several scenarios to take out the operation. No matter how they planned the operation, there were too many variables they could not account for that could cause a drastic failure on their part.

During a break over lunch, James recounted the sniper range event with the team and Chet started laughing. At first, they thought he was laughing at Megan embarrassing the Master Gunny who Chet knew from his days in the Corps, but it was because he had an idea they had not considered. Do not make a direct assault on the location, but three snipers and a couple RPG's might do enough damage to finally cause the local authorities to shut them down. Intelligence reported that the local authorities were taking money and sometimes one of the girls for a night in payment for turning a blind eye to the operation. Make enough noise then the civil authorities will have to act.

One of their biggest concerns was causing the deaths of the girls being held at that location but going back through the intelligence they noticed the girls were not kept there until the night of shipment out of the country. The fact they all missed that point was an embarrassment to one and all which meant they all dove back into the information to insure they didn't miss anything else important.

For two more days they assessed the mission, taking it apart and putting it back together before they came to several critical conclusions. They had no idea how they could get there with the people they felt needed to be on the ground then how to get back out afterwards. The target was not totally isolated, and the consideration of timing so there would be no girls at the location at the time. Equipment was also a concern depending on mode of transportation. The list continued to enlarge as one problem after another cropped up. If this was a pure military operation these problems would be negligible, but this was as Black Ops and those things were critical.

It was James who finally made the statement that even using four men, swimming in, would only have a forty percent chance of success and less than that of survival without major support. Megan knew he wanted to stop the trade of flesh probably worse than anyone but all they would actually be doing was to temporally slow it down until the other side found a new place to operate from. It was logistics that was the killer in the plans. Too many people outside the team had to be in specific places at specific times to support the team which placed the risk of failure too high as far as the team was concerned.

Megan submitted their conclusions and within an hour, they received a stand down. The team broke up heading back to their normal lives knowing they would be reimbursed for their time. The team's final solution for this problem was a political one.

Six months later, the team stopped an attempt to damage the Panama Canal. The mission was a simple one and the team wondered from the beginning why the Panamanian government had not shut the separatists down that was planning to blow up the main Canal Control Center. They learned that several key military leaders of the Panamanian military were involved, and the government did not wish to look as if they were using violence to stop dissent within the country. Tomas rigged an explosive device which the team managed to place in the building the separatists were using as a meeting place and the resulting explosion killed over twenty people in what looked like a gas explosion.

Shortly after they returned from Panama, there was a change of command at Quantico. They had a new Base Commander who brought with him a new Chief of Staff. It took nearly a week before the new command realized they had two officers on the Base that were not subject to staff duties nor was their office subject to the base command. The Chief of Staff contacted a friend of his at Headquarters, Marine Corps who told him that he knew nothing about the Office of Training Analysis.

The Base Sergeant Major tried to assure the Base Commander that the office was a viable asset in the review of training and they had suggested several changes which have proved to be improvements in training. When the General learned that the reports the Office of Analysis submitted were not subject to Command review, he became determined to find out why and put the office in-line with policy. When he found out that the two officers who worked from that office were married with the wife as senior officer, he was determined to have that situation rectified immediately. He called for Major Conley to report immediately to his office. He got James instead.

"Gunner, is there a valid reason why you are in my office instead of Major Conley?" The General asked.

"Yes Sir, the Major is at Albany taking a look at the Supply School, Sir."

"When is she due back?"

"Sir, I have advised the Major of your requirement for her presence and she told me to come in her stead to insure we are prepared to execute your orders, Sir."

"Let me take a guess here. What she probably said was go see what the SOB wants and stall him as much as possible."

"You're only half right General. She said go see what the General wants, not what the SOB wants, Sir."

"Alright, I'll accept that as the truth, now, who do you report to Gunner?"

"The Major Sir."

"Let me rephrase that. Who does your office report too?"

"With all due respect General, but if I am standing here listening to these questions, that means you are not cleared for that information Sir."

"Gunner, the next words out of your mouth better in response to my last question otherwise I'll have your ass in the brig until you are old enough to draw your pension. Do you understand me?"

"Perfectly General. While you call the MP's, may I make a call to insure our daughter is picked up from daycare and taken care of until the Major returns tomorrow, Sir?"

"Get your face out of my officer Mister. When the Major returns, be here with her as soon as she returns and take note, there will be a charge sheet waiting for you and possibly the Major."

"Aye-Aye Sir."

As James left the office he pulled his cell phone from his pocket.

"Did you get all of that Baby?"

"I did Honey, but you sure pushed the envelope on insubordination. Watch your ass James, I'll be home by noon if everything goes alright."

"Okay Baby, be careful and see you tomorrow."

As soon as they hung up Megan made another call and explained the situation. She was told to carry on and the problem would be dealt with. Two hours later the CIA's Deputy Director for Operations walked into the Base Commander's office and left it ten minutes later to return to Langley. When Megan and James reported to the General's office the next day, his attitude was completely different asking them to sit down and then questioning them about any problems they might be having getting cooperation with the training commands. Nothing was said about the previous day's conversation with James or the visit from the Deputy Director.

Contracts

Megan sat looking at the photos of Melissa and Jeff on her office wall considering the conversation she and Jeff had on the way home from Galveston. The subject had come up of having another baby and even getting out of the business of killing. Having another child had crossed her mind many times as Melissa grew older and to have a sibling close enough to her age would give Melissa someone to play with in a couple years. But how to get out of this business considering who was paying the bills was a much more difficult problem.

After Melissa was put to bed, they talked about another baby. Megan said she still had over two weeks of pills left and if James was sure, she would finish those then they could work on having another baby. James told her they should start practicing making a baby tonight and they laughed on their way to the bedroom.

Three days later Megan was reviewing the training schedule for the Camp Pendleton Non-Commissioned Officers Course when the flip phone buzzed in her pocket. Email was all it said, and she opened her coded laptop to see what the email contained. It had an attachment when she opened it she had to take a breath and relax. It was a hit and run accident report involving a motorcycle and a truck. The motorcycle rider was one Tomas J. Garcia of Fort Worth Texas. The truck was stolen and found five miles from the accident site on fire. Tomas was in critical condition at an area hospital. The report noted that he was wearing a helmet and leathers at the time of the accident.

The hairs on the back of Megan's neck tingled demanding answers to the questions, was this just an accident or, had Tomas made an enemy who was trying to take him out or, was this connected to the team's operations? She sent a text to the team stating Tomas was critically injured in a vehicular accident. Accident or on purpose? Watch your six.

Two days later a report came in of Jerome being shot in a failed robbery attempt at the electronic supply house he owned and operated in Jacksonville, Mississippi. Two men had entered the store wearing masks and demanded money. When Jerome told the robbers he only dealt in credit card sales, one of the robbers shot him twice in the chest. Jerome had taken Megan's warning seriously and was wearing a Second Chance vest under his shirt and sports coat he wore at work. The bullets did not penetrate but at close distance, they caused cracked ribs and bruised his heart.

Five days later Howard was shot in a drive by shooting as he was working as a Paramedic in Modesto California. He was attending to the survivors of an earlier drive by at the same scene when the shooters decided to return and do another shooting. He was also wearing body armor under his windbreaker but was hit in the right arm and left leg.

Megan sent a simple three-word text when she read of Howard's injuries. "Go to Ground." This meant for the team to shut off all electronic communications and for everyone to watch their asses.

The hours and days creeped by as Megan awaited news of another attempt on the lives of a team member. It was a week after the attempt on Howard that James's mother was involved in a hit and run accident that shook her up but did not cause her any serious injury. Megan contacted her father and told him they might have to bring Melissa to them and she'd explain in person. That afternoon, he drove down and picked Melissa up. When Megan voiced concern about their safety, her father smiled and told her not to worry. When he pulled out of the drive with her mother sitting in the back seat with Melissa, Megan noticed a sedan pull out in front of his Cadillac then another sedan passed by with two men in it. The passenger in the trail sedan looked at Megan and waved. It was Wild Bill Dedmon. Her father was being escorted by retired Delta Force members.

When Megan walked back into the house, James had their weapons laid out and was checking each one. They had changed their personal weapons before the last operation. They both carried full size Sig P320's with silencers and P320 Compacts as concealed weapons. The H&K MP-5's had been replaced with the silenced Sig MPX. Megan went to pack both of them clothes for a lengthy stay away from the house. James loaded the weapons and their jump bags into her Tahoe then he put their travel bags into the vehicle. These bags had uniforms and other items they might need when out on an inspection tour. Neither had spoken of where they were going but for the time being, it was back to the office, so they could use the coded computers there to begin digging out who was after the team.

Both were wearing body armor as they left the house. She drove her Tahoe as James drove his Denali to the office where Kathy was waiting for them. She had a message from Dotty saying to stand by for movement to the Farm. No other information was provided. An hour later, Master Sergeant Peters arrived with the Base's Provost Sergeant who told them to take what they could carry, and the rest would be loaded into a Suburban from the Provost Marshall's impound lot and taken to the Farm for them. Their vehicles were to stay on Quantico where they would be moved out of sight of the public.

Megan pulled her sniper rifle from the storage room at the office and several other weapons in their cases along with their team field gear also stored there. All they were going to take directly to the Farm were their jump bags and personal weapons. The Provost Sergeant watched as they suited up for a fight in their digitals with silenced pistols and the MPX's hanging from single point slings. They loaded up in the back seat of the Provost Marshall's staff car and were taken to the airfield where they boarded a Marine UH-1Y Venom helicopter and flown to the Farm with a pair of AH-1Z Super Cobras as escort.

Bill Rendell along with William and Clifton from the Dungeon met them at the helicopter pad when they landed and took them to the first house they occupied years ago. Once at the house Bill gave them news that Kevin Short was dead. Shot in the head execution style in his apartment kitchen. U.S. Marshall's had taken James's mother into protective custody and had moved her to a location where they could protect her. As they were talking over coffee, Bill received a text advising that Melissa and her grandparents were safe and sound on Fort Bragg proper in Base Guest Housing. Megan just smiled knowing who would be protecting her parents and daughter.

They went to bed that night with the knowledge that they were being watched over. Megan asked James a question before sleep took them that they both had crawling through their mind. Who had access to the information on the team?

Getting Organized

Megan walked into the living room of the house to find it full of people. The Dungeon crew was there along with Master Sergeant Peters, but there were about a half dozen people she did not know which bothered her. She was dressed casual with her Sig on her hip and ready for anything that may come at her. The one thing that her outward appearance did not show was that she was in a highly pissed off state. There was a slight under current of conversation as she stood looking at the crowd of people in the room as James walked up behind her. Her first words gave no doubt who was in command of the situation.

"Alright knock off the chatter and listen up. Someone has either hacked or has direct access to the system which the syndicate set up and operates out of. Dotty, find the leak and let's plug it soonest. Where is Mark Lucas?"

"Megan, no one knows. I've tried three different ways to contact him. His house is empty, so it looks like he took Denise and the kids underground until the smoke clears." This comment came from Peters.

"Alright, keep looking. Also, who are these other people?"

"There friends of mine Megan." Peters answered her question. "Friends who are not part of the network and who I trust with my life. You move, they move with you and I'll not accept any argument on the subject young lady."

Megan laughed. "Pete, anyone but you or James saying that would have gotten an argument. Any news on my other team members?"

Megan, if you have not received a notice, then we certainly have not either." Dotty replied. "But one thing did come across late last night. The shooters that went after Howard Zimmerman were local talent. Gang bangers for hire. They were found in an old warehouse with bullets in their brains. Whoever is behind this is covering their tracks."

Melvin spoke up. "Megan, how do we know where to look for an intrusion into this syndicates network if we don't know how it works?"

Megan pulled her flip-phone from her pocket and tossed it to Melvin. "Ask them. But remember that except for the phone numbers in that phone for my team the only other aspect common to each of them is payroll. Direct deposits are made each time they were paid. Crack the accounts and follow the money. Someone has accessed that information. Find that someone for me, I'll do the rest."

Dotty stood up and looked around the room before speaking.

"We're setting up in the house next door. Let's go to work people."

Once the room was cleared of the Dungeon crew, James stepped forward and addressed his comments to Peters.

"Top, the woods at the back of the house are a weak point. Last time I was here I walked them as I considered the situation we were in then. You can go all the way to the highway without tripping over anything to dissuade the curious. That hole needs to be plugged soonest."

Peters looked at the men behind him. "Timmons?"

"Got it Top." Timmons motioned to another man and they left the house.

Megan walked up to Peters, put her hands on his shoulders then leaned over and gave him a quick kiss on the lips.

"Pete, you're the best shooter I know, and my father would agree, but you are too old for these kinds of games. Please stay out of harm's way as much as possible."

"I'll try kid, but I'll make no promises." He turned to the door motioning the other men to follow. "Megan, get calm and stay calm. Right now you are too pissed off to tackle this properly. Let Dotty's people do their job. James, I know this is asking a lot, but sit on her if you have to but keep her in the house and out of everyone's hair."

James walked up beside her after everyone had left and wrapped his arm around her shoulder and pulled her close. He could feel her shaking as she rested her head against his shoulder.

"James, I'm scared. I've never been this scared before and I have no control system to guide me through this.

"You have me baby. This scares me too, but we have to get through it and move on. Come on, I'll fix you some waffles."

They were doing the breakfast dishes when Peters walked in the back door accompanied by a stocky black man about Megan's height. Peters went directly to the coffee pot as he did the introductions.

"Megan, James, this is Major Cromwell."

"I've met the Major." James spoke up.

"Yes, good to see you again Gunner and I believe this is your lovely wife, Major Conley that I have heard so much about."

Megan offered her hand. "Major Cromwell, the Major bit is only camouflage. In reality I'm a CIA Field Officer without a field. So please call me Megan."

"Megan, the call I received ordering me down here never mentioned you by anything but Major Conley, therefore, you are a Major and that is that."

"I'm afraid to ask who ordered you down here and why but say your piece and let's get the dog and pony show over with."

Cromwell laughed.

"Megan, in about an hour, two platoons of FAST Company Marines will be landing out in front of these houses to assume responsibility for your protection."

"Who ordered that Major Cromwell?"

Cromwell just looked at Megan as he pulled a small envelope from his rear pocket.

"Also I was asked to give this to you."

Megan accepted the envelope knowing Cromwell was not going to answer her question but only one person in the Corps had the authority to take such action in such a short time. She pulled her switchblade from her back pocket and cut the envelope open. Megan read the note and then smiled at Cromwell.

"Where is he actually at?"

"My quarters on Norfolk, along with Denise and the kids. When you sent the first warning out, he called me about putting them up for a few days. He was packed and ready when you said go to ground. Mark was my Platoon Sergeant back when I was a Second Lieutenant."

"Has he told you what he does for me?"

"No Megan and I never asked him."

"Megan?" Pete spoke up.

"Yes, Pete?"

"Dotty asked me to bring you over once you are ready."

"We can go now Pete. And Pete, I'm sorry if I snapped at you earlier."

"Megan, I can understand your feelings. I've been there myself. But nothing is gained by allowing emotion to gain a good footing."

"Pete I'm still pissed but will work real hard to maintain a reasonable level of calmness."

Pete laughed then motioned towards the back door.

Entering through the back door, Megan noticed the typical undertone of conversation that was always present in the Dungeon. Megan walked up behind Dotty and placed a hand on her shoulder then leaned in close to her ear.

"Dotty, I'm sorry if I came off like a bitch a while ago."

Dotty never turned to look at her as she softly spoke.

"Megan, I actually understand how you are feeling so do not concern yourself with how you acted earlier. Besides, you have established a control over this gaggle of geese which I never could have achieved. Pete is right though. Relax until we need you tough again. We're going to find the people behind this."

"Anything yet?"

"One piece of news that just came in a few minutes ago that is not encouraging. They went after Jake Grainger this morning, just before daylight."

"How bad?"

"Three dead, one wounded on their side. Whoever they were, they under estimated who they were going after. Two got away but ran into Sam who shot up their vehicle causing them to crash. He snatched them up and took them back to Jake's place. That's all we know right now."

"Do I know Sam?"

"No, he was one of Jake's team."

"Dotty!! We have an incoming video communication!" Gretchen called out.

"Open it up on the big screen and everyone be quiet!" Dotty commanded.

When the screen opened, it was Jake Grainger on the other end.

"Dotty, I don't have much time so here it is. The crew sent after me are South African Mercs. The survivors claim not to know who hired them except the price was high. Sam is questioning them right now. They tried to confuse the issue by speaking Afrikaner, but Sam also speaks the language. Anyway, my own team is converging now except for Denise and we've lost contact with her."

"Jake, Denise and Mark are safe, but I'll not divulge their location."

"Thanks Megan, I understand. We're circling our wagons here. It's all on you Megan. This is your battle to fight."

"I understand Jake. Take care of yourself. We'll do the heavy lifting but don't get too comfortable in case I need a hand."

"We'll do what we can. Grainger out."

With that he cut the connection and the monitor went to black. Megan stood thinking for a minute before she finally spoke.

"Dotty, have you connected with the syndicate yet?"

"Not sure who we've talked to but yes. Why?"

"Send the following message. Tiger Lily suspects actual attempt is being made to shut down the syndicate not just her team. Advise all members to become aware of danger and to take precautions. Notify this team of any suspicions or attempts of harm immediately."

"Gretchen did you get that?" Dotty asked.

"Yes, and it is going out now."

"So Megan, your code name is Tiger Lily? Cute and it fits."

"Dotty as far as I know I've never had a code name with the syndicate. Tyler, give Gretchen's message ten minutes then start looking for any comment referring to Tiger Lily across the net. Let's see where it leads us."

"You got it Megan." Tyler replied.

Dotty laughed and went back to work as Megan and James just moved around the room watching the crew work. Cromwell walked up beside Megan.

"Major I would suggest you change into digitals before the troops arrive. It would behoove you to greet your troops in uniform."

"My troops? I thought you were in command?"

"No Megan, once on the ground, you are in command. I issued orders to the Platoon Commanders to report to you and that you were in command. I'm out of here in about three minutes and the Marines are loading up right now in CH-53's. The clock is running."

Megan and James returned to their house and changed into their digitals complete with body armor and vests. Megan had her silenced Sig P320 in a leg drop holster and her P320 Compact on her vest. On her left hip was a four-magazine pouch for her MPX which was hanging from a single point sling in front of her. James checked her appearance before letting her out of the house as they heard the big helicopters coming in to land. They left the house to meet the troops.

The first helicopter landed with the ramp descending and it had hardly touched down when the first Marine was leaping off the ramp and moving towards the houses ready for a fight if one erupted. The helicopter was lifting within a minute of touching down and cleared the landing zone for the next bird to land. After the second helicopter had lifted, the Platoon Commanders gathered their platoons and fell them in formation then turned the formation over to their platoon sergeants. The two officers then joined and went to Megan's position came to attention in front of her and both saluted her which she returned.

"Gentlemen, that will be the last time anyone salutes me or any officer during this attachment. Am I clear on that gentlemen?"

"Aye-Aye Major." They both echoed.

"Who is senior here?"

"I am Major."

"Fine Lieutenant Cohill. You are now my Executive Officer. Lieutenant Dandridge, grab your radio operators and bring them to the house behind me on my right. Have the Platoon Sergeants move the men into shaded areas until we can get organized." She turned to James. "Gunner, once the men are out of the sun take the Platoon Sergeants for a nature walk. Show them the back forty and watch out for Timmons and his people. And if you do see him, tell him I need to see him."

"You got it Major." James commented with a grin.

"Oh, and gentlemen, Gunner Conley is my husband if the names confuses anyone."

"We were already aware of that Major." Dandridge commented. "May I ask where he is in the chain of command?"

"He's not unless you wish to consider him our First Sergeant."

"Sounds like a plan Major. I guess we had best be getting busy." Cohill commented.

Megan gave the Lieutenant's the basic plan and let them develop their guard plan knowing the abilities of the men they commanded. She made it clear to the Lieutenant's she did not

192

have their knowledge and was only in de facto command. Megan sat down with both Lieutenants and worked on the logistics of keeping the men supplied with rations and other items of comfort.

Feeding the Marines was on top of Megan's priority list, so she contacted Major Cromwell who arranged for a field kitchen complete with cooks to be moved on site. James voiced a concern about someone screwing with the rations, poisoning the men so they could not perform their duties. Dotty arranged for the rations to be brought in from the Agency's own kitchen for the Marine cooks to prepare.

That evening Tyler reported a dozen communications referencing Tiger Lily's comments about destroying the syndicate. Mel was slowly taking the syndicates payroll system apart piece by piece, but it was slow going tracking all the ins and outs of how it was set up. The money was filtered into offshore banks then filtered again into the bank accounts of those requiring funds to accomplish the tasks needing the funds.

Gamers??

One aspect of waiting is the tension of the people who must fight the fight. Megan and James were able to burn off some of the tension late at night but knowing that sitting around just added to the tension, they came up with an exercise plan that no one argued with. Each morning they ran with two squads of Marines, dressed as they were inside the squads as if they were members of the squads.

Six days after moving to the Farm, Kathy showed up with a couple of men that gave both the Farm's Security personal and the Marines a bit of trouble until James went to the main gate and identified them. Chet Walker and Jim Tillman had met up and slowly made their way to Virginia after the call went out to go to ground. They had gotten onto Quantico using the U.S. Marshall's identification that Chet had kept from their first mission and went to the offices finding only Kathy.

Kathy was uncertain about the authenticity of Chet's credentials or the tale they told but figured once at the gate, either they would be properly identified, or security would arrest them. Two days later Jerome was brought to the Farm under protection of U.S. Marshalls. Tomas was recovering his injuries as was Howard and they had both been moved to military hospitals to further protect them.

Dotty's people were working around the clock trying to find that one thread they needed to pull which might unravel the web woven through the internet to expose the people behind the plot to destroy the syndicate. As each string was pulled, it was noticed that the only people referring to Tiger Lily were not direct members of the syndicate based upon the information already gleaned from the hours of research.

Megan didn't have much to do while waiting for an answer they could set plans to, so she did what she remembered her father talking about as she was growing up as an Army brat. She toured the Marines positions both day and night checking on the men under her de facto command. She was always completely geared up for a fight and the men often asked about the weapons she carried.

The Marines were broken down into four sections: the On-duty section; the Reaction Force; the Stand-by section; and the Off Duty section. Training never stopped for these Marines and she spent time on the ranges with them showing them the weapons she carried were not just for show. The Marines became familiar with her entire Team as they followed her example visiting with the Marines and spending time on the ranges with them.

Megan arranged to have one of the classrooms converted into a theater for use by the off-duty section along with snacks, non-alcoholic refreshments and a beer ration of one per man. She let it known, that any non-drinker caught supplying his buddy with additional alcohol would stand before her for discipline. Also, each man submitted three movie titles they would like to see and that list was culled of duplicates and the movies obtained for viewing on the large eighty-inch television. The only other requirement she made was that every individual would be armed at all times, even when off duty.

Lieutenant Cohill proved to be an excellent Executive Officer in insuring laundry and other sundry items were dealt with in an efficient manner. Kathy had stayed once at the Farm and it was not long before she hooked up with Lieutenant Dandridge which added a bit of comic relief as they tried to hide their off-time exercises.

Dotty had to schedule time for the married members of the Dungeon crew time with their families in order to release the tension of being sequestered for the long hours they were spending on this problem. The families themselves were being protected by CIA Security personal with the children being taken to and from their schools. Dotty commented to Megan that she would hate to see the overtime bill for this project.

Time was running out as they watched the stock market slowly drop as a result of members of the syndicate backing out of projects and investments. Tyler was seeing an increase in both verbal and internet communications between syndicate members as they wondered who was behind this attack on their system. It did not help that one member had suffered a heart attack and another had a stroke during this time. Was it the stress on the syndicate or just fate that played a hand already dealt before this situation occurred?

Mel finally pulled a thread that lead to the payment of the Afrikaners who had attacked Jake. It came from the syndicate's system, but the authorization code was from a syndicate member who had died before Megan had entered the system. But it did give them an ISP to work with and Mel spent long hours taking it apart until he had a specific location, an address to give to Megan.

Megan had the information passed on to the FBI to put the address under surveillance before any attempt to move on it was determined. Two days later the FBI knocked on the door of a single resident home. They found what would be considered a normal family; father, mother, and two children; a boy and girl. The boy was fourteen and very intelligent with high computer skills.

The investigation turned up a plot executed online by gamers that thought they were playing a game not knowing the real reason behind it. The young man the FBI interviewed showed the investigators the game and how to access it. Connor, as the young man was named, was sent to the Farm along with is mother to sit down with Tyler and Mel to show them the game and how it worked and who the different players were. Within forty-eight hours, Tyler had taken the game apart and back traced the key players for the FBI. Seven players were given to the CIA to track down as they were out of the country.

It took Tyler and Mel a week to finally pin down the origin of the game. When Mel announced the location of the server providing the game a scramble for a World Atlas was on. The location was on the Island of Bonaire in the Leeward Antilles in the Caribbean Sea off the coast of Venezuela. The island was once part of the Netherlands Antilles and was now considered a special municipality of the Netherlands.

Megan went to work planning a mission to retrieve the server or destroy it if it could not be quickly removed and transported off the island. Howard had joined them two days earlier but as he said upon arrival, his shooting arm was not up to even the lowest standards. He was shooting daily, but no one disputed his reasons for opting out of the mission. The delicate part of the mission was this was to a friendly country with tourist traffic, especially scuba divers. Jerome suggested a recon to confirm the location but considering that every member of the team had been targeted for death, it was a possibility any of the scuba trained members might be spotted.

James came up with a solution and contacted the SEAL Command at Norfolk. Four hours later three SEALs reported to the Farm for their mission. Twenty-four hours later they were on their way to Bonaire as tourists to dive the reefs of the island. A week later they returned with over a hundred photos of their time on the island and diving. It took a while to sort through the photos to isolate the twenty-two photos that were important to the mission. There was a guard on the rear door of a dive supply house where the server was located. Power cables and phone cables were thick going into the building along with a pair of air conditioners to keep the server cool in the arid climate of the island.

Megan developed three methods of hitting the server which to the team all looked good. All they had to do was determine which was the best for the mission. James upset Megan when he quietly told her she was not going on the mission. When she challenged his statement, he tossed a report on the table stating the Zika virus was showing signs of infiltrating the Caribbean areas and if she wanted another baby, she was staying home. When she further protested, the entire team put their foot down agreeing with James on the matter. Megan finally submitted but James knew they would have this out again later when alone.

Planning for the mission went on with Megan being the team leader but operational control going to Jerome and James. Their plans were nearly complete and ready to submit for logistical support when fate lent a hand. A member of the Dutch government along with a Captain from the Dutch Marines arrived to assist in the retrieval of the server. It was important to them as much it was to Megan that this situation be resolved as quick as possible.

The plan was radically altered with the team consisting of Jerome, James, Tyler and Melvin assisted by a squad of Royal Dutch Marines under the command of the Major. Tyler and Mel were included in order that the server was properly shut down and disconnected. Tyler and Mel were taken to the pistol range to prove to the Major they could defend themselves if needed. Both proved to the Major they were capable of defending themselves with a handgun.

Twenty-four hours later they were aboard a Dutch warship briefing the ship's Captain and the detachment of Marines on board to their mission. As they drew close to the island in the middle of the night, two Zodiacs with the raiding party slipped away towards the beach as the ship headed for the docks. Once docked, two trucks would be commandeered by Marines and driven to the target to collect the raiding party and the servers.

The guard was taken without trouble and entry into the server's area was only slowed down by the double locks on the door. No attempt was made to shut it down until Jerome had carefully examined the two servers found within the room for booby traps. Tyler also examined it carefully as Mel focused on the power cables and other lines. Mel hooked into the server and found there was an auxiliary phone line leading into it connected to a local phone.

It took some doing but Mel was able to isolate the phone to a residence in Sabana, a suburb of Kralendijk. The Dutch Major had a long talk with the guard who was more than willing to tell the raiders anything he knew. He was only paid to watch the building and if a red light came on over the door to call a phone number and someone would come to fix the problem. The guard said this had only happened once and it was because a fuse had blown causing the server to lose power. Mel pulled the fuse and the guard called the phone number.

Twenty minutes later a car pulled up to the back of the dive house and a man fitting the description the guard gave them exited and went directly to the door. The guard played his part well knowing he was not going to prison as promised by the Major. When the man entered the server's room he was met by Jerome and James who had him cuffed and under their control within seconds of entering the room. Frisking him they found he was carrying an illegal firearm that had been made in China.

The individual was carrying papers stating he was from Nationalist China, Taiwan who spoke excellent Dutch. The Major along with James, Tyler, and Mel took the man's car and drove to the suspect's house. They found a prostitute who was waiting for the suspect to return that could tell them nothing more than they were interrupted before their deal was done and she was waiting for him to return to finish the appointment and pay her.

They found the room in the house where his computer was located along with extensive files on Megan and the teams. Even though none of them could read the writing, they agreed it was not Chinese. James took a photo with his cell phone and sent it to Megan. Five minutes later she replied it was Korean. Dotty sent a message two minutes later telling them to leave everything intact and a team of Korean language experts would be there within twelve hours to take over the house and the computer. Tyler was to stay at the house until relieved and civilian clothing would be brought for him. The prostitute was told she would be paid one thousand dollars to keep her mouth shut which she was more than happy to agree too and was told the money would be there the next evening.

The Major sent two Marines to the house to insure Tyler had protection in case there was another individual on the island that might come to the house and cause Tyler harm. The server was placed back on-line, and the trucks were sent back to the ship with the rest of the Marine detachment as the Zodiacs were taken to the ship by their coxswains. Jerome and James along with Mel changed into civilian clothing on ship and returned to the Farm on the first flight out of the islands airport.

One More Thread To Pull

James returned to find Megan sullen and a bit standoffish. He could tell she was still mad about being left out of the mission to Bonaire but that night she all but attacked him in the shower before going to bed. She told James before they went to sleep that once this operation is over, she was quitting the work for the syndicate, if there was still a syndicate to work for and she was going to have another baby as soon as they could make one.

The next morning Megan pulled the files on the initial Korean operation that brought her and James together and began to review the information. Somewhere within those files had to be a connection they had missed the first time. They had prevented a war but there was something more to this that maybe in preventing that war they had overlooked.

By the end of the week, every scrap of paper had arrived from the house on Bonaire along with the individual operating the systems. Taiwan's Intelligence Service was able to confirm he was not from Taiwan but could not determine who he was. He was a ghost within the intelligence community. But when he finally broke, he spoke a North Korean dialect which gave the CIA something to work with.

It took nearly three weeks before Tyler cracked the hidden files on the Korean agent's computer. He had the help of the Korean language people due to how the files were configured. Deep within the files was an email file with an ISP in the United States. The emails were coded but all of the codes they tried to open the emails failed. They finally determined a one-time code was used for each email and without a key, they would stay locked.

Dotty's people focused on the ISP as the Agency's Cryptologists worked on the emails. Megan asked for the Embassy staff files for that time frame and began to work on each individual to see if there was a connection. James told her to include the Marine Detachment to insure no one was left out.

As Megan was running the embassy and Marine staff, double checking timelines and associations, Mel found a glitch in the payroll activity of the syndicate. He spent hours on the glitch working it backwards looking at the money transfers until he came to what he estimated was the first payment to an offshore account. Tyler was working the gaming information and together they were able to tag the disbursement of funds as one of the first the gamers ever made. But who was the owner of the account?

Dotty finally had to order both Tyler and Mel to stand down for forty-eight hours because they were both becoming obsessed with finding the answers to the problems they were working on. James had to make Megan take some time off and they slipped up to visit with Melissa for a weekend. The feeling that since the Korean agent was no longer contracting hits on the team members, it was safe to make such a trip and Megan's parents had returned to their farm with Melissa. Jeff took Melissa fishing at the farm's pond before they returned to the teams and went back to work.

Back at the Farm, Megan asked Ron to do some looking into the bank accounts of a half dozen of the embassy staff since Mel was tied up with the syndicate's accounts. The only thing he found from that time period was the activity on Cecil Owens account to an on-line trading firm. Cecil Owens had been the senior CIA Field Officer at the embassy, Megan's boss. Getting the information concerning the trades was difficult and required a Federal Warrant to access those trades. Ron looked as far back into Owens' banking activities as possible, five year's worth of banking finding he had been playing the market for years.

Owens had retired two years ago and was living in Washington State. His banking activity did not show anything extraordinary including the small royalties on his stock purchases. Until they were able to access the trading site and learn what stocks were being purchased, they were stalled at looking at Owens. They set him aside and moved on to others from the embassy.

The leadership sat down and looked hard at the conditions they were living and working under and determined that since the server was now in their hands the risk to their lives had been greatly diminished. The Marines were sent back to Norfolk after a formation was held with Megan giving thanks to the Marines for their efforts on the teams behalf. She walked the ranks and thanked each one of the Marines before they loaded up on trucks for the return to Norfolk.

The Dungeon was packed up and returned to Langley leaving Megan's team at the Farm. Megan sent the team to the Lodge as they returned to Quantico. Kathy returned to the office after a long weekend with Dandridge. It was also during this time the Cryptologists finally figured out the coding system. The Korean had six English language books in his library with a number written in Korean in the upper right corner of the front of the book. Comparing it to the coded emails showed that number as the first number in the number groupings telling the receiver of the message which book to use. Soon they were decoding the messages confirming the fact the Korean was using the game to hire and pay for the hits on Megan's team.

Megan was still thinking someone at the embassy was involved, but had eliminated all but Owens. She had Tyler send a message that the Tiger Lily was operational and on the prow. Within twelve hours and message was sent to the Korean's special email instruction him to offer a quarter-million dollars for Megan's death. Tyler looked at the sent email files to see how the Korean had answered other emails and copied the reply back.

Mel finally received the information he needed and spent long hours breaking the stock purchases and sales until he found a pattern. But one stock stood out that was purchased but never sold, even when it was losing money. The company was called Armament Components and they produced parts for military weapon systems. According to their website, they had an improved laser guided system that could be programed to detonate the bomb as an air burst greatly increasing the killing radius of the weapon.

Mel asked Ron to background the owners of Armament Components, cross referencing them against Owens and they hit pay dirt. Lincoln Meyers, the founder of Armament Components had roomed with Owens their last two years at Stanford. Phone records dating back before Owens was posted to Korea were requested to see how much communication between the two men had taken place.

Megan asked that the phone records of the Korean be compared to the records of Bruno Hochbauer and his PA Carl Harris. Harris's computer was destroyed in the explosion that nearly killed James, so they were unable to find if any emails to the Korean came from him, but she asked to check to see if any emails from the Korean were ever sent to the ISP's that serviced Harris from the different locations he was known to have been in as Hochbauer's PA.

Time is measured in seconds, minutes, hours, and days except when a person is waiting for the other shoe to drop. The FBI had Owens under surveillance, but he had yet to do anything out of the ordinary to arouse suspicion of any wrong doing. Megan and James flew to Hawaii to survey Marines training at several locations, plus they enjoyed some quiet beach time before heading back to file their reports.

Two days after their return from Hawaii, Megan was called to Langley and was taken directly into the Director's Office. The Director told Megan once this problem had been dealt with she had to decide which side she was on. He further stated that since he had become aware of the syndicate's activities he would have to do something about shutting them down since they were operating outside of political control. When Megan inquired about possible future assignments within the Agency, the Director tried to ignore the question but when pushed became very vague in his answer. Megan returned to Quantico more determined than ever to leave the CIA once this problem was solved.

The Cryptologists working with the Dungeon were moving things forward at a pace that was quickening to its final resolution.

The further they went back into the emails the more the evidence was building against Cecil Owens for treason along with conspiracy to commit murder of a Federal Agent. They just did not have the final string to connect the emails directly to Owens. They finally connected five emails to the Korean from the Carl Harris character prior to his death. The second email had the payment codes attached.

Sweeping the hard drives of the game server, they found the photos of the team expressed as villains within the game. The photo backgrounds were altered to make them look like game specific photos along with code names. James laughed when he saw Megan's game description as a Chinese secret agent posing as a prostitute. James's character was portrayed as Megan's pimp.

The final thread was pulled when a segment of a deleted email was discovered between Harris and the Korean mentioning Owens. Megan notified Dotty that Owens might be the key but who is behind the others. She wanted him to run, hopefully to a place where they could find the handler for the Korean agents. The team was at the Lodge and she put them on a four-hour notice. The FBI who were watching Owens were warned they were going to try to spook him into running and the FBI planted a tracking device on his vehicles to assist in keeping track of him.

Megan arranged for a C-17 out of Pope Air Force Base to take them where ever they had to go in order to bring this project to a conclusion. They drove to Megan's parents with Melissa and waited until they received the word on Owens actions. Tyler coded a message to Owens from Megan and sent it through the server as if he was the Korean. He added a code to the email that transmitted the email back through the system once it was opened which would give them notice of time when Owens would see the message. Tyler also set a photo of Megan on the game site with her laughing. Two hours after he sent the email, Tyler received acknowledgement that the email had been received. And it was opened on Owens ISP.

Events began to move quickly as the FBI reported Owens leaving his house with a single bag. He drove to Seattle, rented a car and drove south. Megan called the air field and was told the C-17 was readied and waiting for her arrival. Megan and Jeff had changed into Army uniforms since they were borrowing a C-17 and when they arrived at Pope they were greeted by eight rough looking men geared for action. These were Delta Force operators who placed themselves under her command for the duration of the operation. Megan ordered the C-17 to Air Force Academy where she was going to pick up the rest of her team.

The FBI were able to place a tracking device on Owens's rented car during a stop at a Denny's Restaurant where he also made use of their Wi-Fi and bought a plane ticket to Seoul, Korea. Megan consulted with the C-17's pilot while on the ground in Colorado Springs about any special requirements for making the hop to Korea. They flew to Hickam Field where they picked up an additional flight crew then began hop scotching across the Pacific towards Korea. The FBI managed to hold Owens plane on the ground for an additional hour for mechanical problems giving Megan's aircraft the additional time even though they had already left Hawaii and were well ahead of him. There was also a female FBI agent out of the Los Angeles office on the airplane to assist in keeping track of him. She got off at Guam and a male agent boarded for the trip to Japan then Korea.

End Game

Three of the Delta operators were of Asian descent and were waiting for Owens at Kimpo Airport at Seoul. Megan had gone directly to the embassy upon landing in Korea to inform the Ambassador of the situation and her purpose in Korea. He told her he had received a special message from the State Department informing him of her mission and to be ready to support the mission and also to be ready to inform the Korean Government if necessary. He had a packet to present to the Korean Government if necessary advising them of the threat by outside forces to start a war with the North. He only asked her to be as discreet as possible but to put a stop to this treachery.

Owens was followed to the apartment of a known prostitute who was known to service wealthy businessmen who visited Seoul. An hour later a Korean male also visited the apartment and when he left, he had Owens bag. This individual was followed to another apartment then about forty-five minutes later he left with the bag and went to the Inchon docks where he placed the bag on a fishing boat. Four of the Delta team had followed behind the individual and when he left the docks he was snatched before he could get to his car. Megan and her team caught up with the team at the docks and called for the Marine Security Detachments Bomb Dog.

The fishing boat was quietly boarded and the crew taken then the bomb dog went to work. Beneath the bunk Owens bag was sitting on was located four pounds of RDX rigged to a cell phone as a detonator. Delta's explosive expert easily disarmed the bomb and left it on the bunk. The boats crew was isolated below decks under guard as they waited. The tail on Owens reported he had left the prostitutes apartment and was heading towards Inchon. The other two Asian Delta operators had changed into clothing they had found on the boat and took places on the boat as crew.

Owens arrived in a cab and went directly to the boat where he was shown the small cabin he was to occupy. When he stepped into the cabin he found himself looking at Megan sitting on a small stool in the corner with her silenced Sig P320 in her hand pointed at him.

"Come on in Cecil, we need to talk."

"Are you here to kill me Megan?"

"It is tempting Cecil, considering you have contracted to have me killed along with my husband, and possibly my daughter if she found herself in the line of fire. That in itself gives me a great cause to put a bullet in you, but no, I shall not as long as you cooperate."

"Cooperate? And go back to the states to be hung for treason?"

"Cecil, you are already dead. Look at the bunk. That was under your bunk and is rigged to be detonated by a cell phone. Whoever you thought was going to protect you from the hangman intended to insure you could never be used against them."

"Bullshit, you planted that in order to scare me into talking. It's not going to work."

Megan sighed.

"Cecil standing behind you is my husband. Be very still as he insures you do not have any means of hurting yourself or any of us. And consider this, he is extremely protective of our daughter and the only reason he has not already killed you is because I asked him not to, but if you try to fight him, all bets are off, and he is very capable of killing you with his bare hands."

The grin on Megan's face sent a chill up Owens spine.

James nearly stripped Owens insuring he was incapable of causing harm before handcuffing him and leading him off the boat onto the docks where he was handed over to the Delta Operators. As the Delta team moved off the dock, Korean Marines arrived with the current CIA Field Officer from the embassy. They took the crew off the boat and examined the charts finding a rendezvous location already marked on the chart. Two squads of Korean Marines took the boat to sea to meet whoever was to meet Owens as Megan and her entire crew headed back to the C-17 waiting for them to return them to the United States. Owens was shocked when he boarded the C-17 to find the prostitute and the Korean contact who had taken his bag to the boat.

When the Korean Marines reached the location on the chart, they observed another fishing boat moving towards them. They had placed the cell phone with the blasting cap on the rear deck of the boat away from the main charge and as the other fishing boat closed on theirs, the phone rang and the blasting cap detonated charring the deck where it was lying. The Marines turned their boat to close with the other and a gun battle resulted as they closed then boarded the other craft. One Marine was killed and two others wounded as they secured the other boat having to kill each crewman that had resisted them. They took photos of the other crew and stripped the boat of anything which might provide intelligence then scuttled it before returning to Inchon. North Korea never commented on their missing intelligence gathering fishing boat or its crew.

Cecil Owens had invested heavily in Armament Components realizing that the weapons system would be vital to the defense of South Korea in a war with the North. When relations between the two countries cooled, he knew he was liable to lose most of his investment. His wife had left him when she found out about his investments and how it was going to affect their lives once he retired. He had met the prostitute through one of his Field Agents and was deep into recovering his losses by arranging the shipment of drugs into the South before he realized he had been doped by North Korean agents.

He felt he had no way out except to continue to assist in the drug smuggling especially once he learned the agents were prepping the country for takeover by the North. Owens figured he could control events and even recover his investments until Megan entered the picture and reported the missing Field Agents that he knew had been killed to hide the drug smuggling. He set up the attack on her at the warehouse to remove her curiosity concerning the missing Field Agents through his contact who had advised him of the syndicate and the man they had working from inside of it.

Cecil Owens would spend the rest of his life in prison for his crimes against the country of his birth. The information he provided broke the resistance of the unknown Korean from Bonaire then with his information the CIA broke the Korean handler. The prostitute was returned to South Korea where she provided pages of information which not only resulted in the collapse of the smuggling ring but nearly a dozen North Korean agents working in the South. She was later executed once she had no value left to Korean Intelligence.

The two North Korean agents were also returned to South Korea where they were not as helpful as the prostitute. They were also executed and buried in unmarked graves.

A New Life & Reassignment

Megan and James had a decision to make concerning their future. They had enough money in Melissa's college fund to provide her with a good education and if they sold the Lodge, they could also provide a good education for another child which they had started trying to have as soon as they returned to Quantico. James was obligated to remain in the Marine Corps and once they severed the ties with the CIA, he would probably be reassigned duties befitting his rank. He was being carried as an Infantry Warrant seconded to Intelligence. Megan told James she would be proud to just be the wife of a Marine and she'd find something to do to help with the loss of income from her leaving government employment. Megan told him she could always teach languages at whatever schools were near where he was stations.

Megan transmitted her resignation from the CIA through proper channels and waited. Each morning they opened their office with Kathy still acting as their secretary and tried to find plenty of work to stay busy as they waited for her termination papers and orders.

A week after she had sent in her resignation, she received via a courier, a bankbook with a deposit slip for five million dollars along with a note only saying 'for services rendered'. When she posted a question concerning the money to the syndicates system, nothing came back except a message that the address could not be found. The syndicate had dismantled their network, or so she thought. The next day FedEx Overnight delivered a package containing a new phone and laptop. In the package was also a note telling her to put the money to good use and the IRS would not require taxes on the money, only the interest.

James applied for thirty days leave and they took Melissa to the Lodge for her first trip to the mountains. James took Melissa fishing in the small streams that ran through the property for trout and at night he and Megan worked hard at making another child.

Three weeks into their first real vacation, a conga line of vehicles came up the mountain to the Lodge. This at first frightened both Megan and James as they stood looking out the front windows with their MPX's in hand and Melissa in the basement with the couple that took care of the Lodge while they were away. Dotty, Dave and Jake Grainger got out of the first vehicle causing the tension Megan and James was feeling to flow out of their bodies.

The next vehicle contained the Commandant of the Marine Corps along with a couple of other senior officers. Civilians exited the next two vehicles and once gathered up they walked up the path from the parking area to the house. Megan had her MPX on its single point sling and just moved it to her back as she opened the front door and stepped out onto the porch. James had his in his left hand and just let it hang muzzle down so as not to be a threat. Jake laughed at the image of them armed as he took the steps two at a time with his hand out in greeting.

Introductions were made by Jake on the porch as each individual entered the Lodge. James collected Megan's MPX and took both of them to their room and secured them before letting the couple with Melissa know everything was alright and they could come up. Being this was a former ski lodge the living room had plenty of room for everyone although a couple chairs had to be brought from the dining room so all could have a seat.

It was the Commandant who opened the conversation.

"Major Conley, what are your plans now that you have resigned from the CIA?"

"Sir, I believe my rank as Major is null and void now Sir. It's just Megan now or if you wish, Mrs. Conley."

"Gunner Conley, is she always this dense or was I not clear?"

"General, she is far from dense, but I have to admit I may have missed something here."

The Commandant chuckled then looked at Jake.

"Think I was a bit ambiguous?"

"Just a bit Franklin, why don't you try it again."

"Megan, if you desire to remain in the Corps as a Major in Intelligence while the Gunner completes his enlistment, you may do so, but I cannot guarantee you will not be separated from time to time as he or even you travels overseas for duty. Your date of entry into the Corps will be the date you entered government service with the CIA and your date of rank will stay as it was when you were frocked with gold oak leaves. Is that clear enough?"

"Very clear Commandant, but I may be pregnant with our second child, or at least I hope I am Sir."

"That is not a problem and I do believe we can prevent the Gunner from an overseas tour until after the child is born and he had time to spoil it before he must report. Which brings up his future. Gunner you are qualified for Recon although I do believe a FAST Company could use your experience. With your medals, you would look a bit silly being an engineer where I believe was where you started before you were selected for State Department duty. You get this one choice this one-time Gunner."

"A FAST Company is fine with me stateside Sir. I'll go where I'm needed overseas, even a kitchen if that is where I'm needed the most Sir."

The General reached into his trousers pocket and pulled a twenty-dollar bill from it and handed it to Jake.

"I should have learned a couple decades ago about betting against you Jake. You called it. He is all Marine for sure."

Jake took the bill then smiled as he looked at James and Megan.

"General, if you do not mind. I think this couple belongs in MARSOC instead of a FAST Company. Their knowledge of special operations and intelligence would greatly benefit that command."

"Yes Jake, I think it would be a better assignment for them. Round peg in Ye Old Round Hole.   Major Conley, any comments?"

"No General. It sounds like a better plan overall."

"Senator, you have something to say?" The Commandant inquired.

The civilian who had used a cane to walk leaned forward in his chair and smiled.

"Both of you will receive several medals for your actions and leadership during this period of crisis. It is all this government can do in thanks for the effort and dedication to duty both of you have shown. There is still a lot to do in keeping this country safe and we'd like the both of you to continue working as you have been doing."

"No Senator." James spoke up.

"Excuse me Gunner?"

"I said no. Megan decided before we ever went back to Korea she was leaving the business. I not only agree with her but support her completely. I'll go anywhere ordered and do the job I am ordered to do, but I will not stand by having my wife and the mother of my children placed at risk again. Commandant, if she is placed at risk in the line of normal duties, I shall not question that action but no more black ops."

"Gunner Conley you remind me of a Gunner who once told me I was an idiot just minutes before I had my leg blown off. I should have listened to him but I'm hearing what you just said loud and clear. Megan, please destroy the laptop you received at Quantico and you will never be bothered again by us.

"Senator, I have the laptop and cell phone here if you would care to take them with you."

"Thank you, I shall?"

"So Megan, do you wish to take my offer and stay in the Corps with the Gunner?" The Commandant asked.

Megan looked at James and smile, replying as she looked at him.

"Yes General, I shall stay as long as he stays. But only as long as our children do not need us more than the Corps."

"Then we have a few documents to sign and a few medals to award before we leave. Colonel Marlow, the brief case please."

The Commandant's senior aide presented the General with a briefcase and as he was opening it Megan asked another question.

"General, what will our assignment be now?"

"You will maintain your Office of Training Analysis until your next child is six months old then the Gunner will get to visit far off places for a year then both of you will be reassigned. Will this be a problem for the two of you?"

"No Sir."

"Good, now let's get this over with. I know a great steakhouse in Denver and I believe the Senator is buying."

"Megan, Kathy will stay as your secretary until you close that office. Is that alright with you?" Dotty questioned.

"No problem Dotty, thank you."

An hour later they were once again alone at the Lodge and James asked Megan a question he had in his mind early in the meeting.

"Honey, are you pregnant?"

"James Darling, if the over the counter test is correct, yes, as of yesterday morning I'm pregnant."

"Fantastic!"

About the Author

Leon Michaels is the author of several novels and short stories that reflect his twenty-three years of military service.   Michaels enlisted in the Marine Corp in 1970 and has memberships in the Veterans of Foreign Wars, the American Legion, the Disabled American Veterans organizations, NRA, and Rotary International. In 1971, he married his high school sweetheart, raised three daughters and has three grandsons. He calls Creek County, Oklahoma home.

24057250R00133

Made in the USA
Columbia, SC
18 August 2018